She smiled at him.

John offered her a nut from the glass tray between them and then took one himself, his strong white teeth biting with evident enjoyment. 'I want to know all kinds of things about you. But if you don't want to talk that's fine.'

It was a generous-minded offer, she decided, and sat in silence for a while to consider it. 'What if there are things in my past I don't want to talk about?' she asked.

'Then by all means don't talk about them. But it's been my experience that a lot of things people keep secret are less frightening when they're talked about.'

Gill Sanderson is a psychologist who finds time to write only by staying up late at night. Weekends are filled by her hobbies of gardening, running and mountain walking. Her ideas come from her work, from one son who is an oncologist, one son who is a nurse and her daughter who is a trainee midwife. She first wrote articles for learned journals and chapters for a textbook. Then she was encouraged to change to fiction by her husband, who is an established writer of war stories.

Recent titles by the same author:

A FAMILY FRIEND*
A FAMILY AGAIN*
A FAMILY TO SHARE*

* Loving Sisters trilogy

UNDO THE PAST

BY
GILL SANDERSON

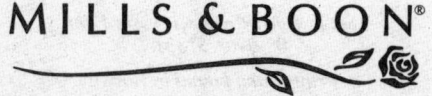

For David—a biologist who cared for children.

First published in Great Britain 1999
Harlequin Mills & Boon Limited,
Eton House, 18-24 Paradise Road, Richmond, Surrey TW9 1SR

© Gill Sanderson 1999

ISBN 0 263 81523 4

Set in Times Roman 10½ on 12 pt.
03-9904-51331-D

Printed and bound in Norway
by AIT Trondheim AS, Trondheim

CHAPTER ONE

'I WAS told to phone Larry—' the voice sounded perplexed '—because Larry was the one who knew everything about one of our patients—a Brian Hughes. I'm afraid I'm not making much progress with him. Do you know where Larry is?'

She liked the voice. It was unusually deep, but had a gentle, caressing quality about it. It was slow and soft, too, and she wondered if this man ever raised it in anger. She suspected not. This man—

Abruptly she remembered that this was a professional call. She'd just come off duty after a particularly tiring stint, but obviously she would still help if she could. 'My name's Laura McLeod,' she said, 'Sister Laura McLeod. But for some reason I get called Larry.'

'Ah, I see. I'm John Hawke. I've just joined Dr Miller's firm as Paediatric Specialist Registrar. And I think that the name Laura sounds much more attractive than Larry.'

'Sounds?' she queried.

'I like sounds. I like the sound of *Swan Lake* that I can hear coming from your room. There's a danger in medicine that we look too much and don't listen enough.'

Laura wriggled herself further up the bed and turned down the volume on her stack. This was an unexpectedly interesting conversation. And she liked talking to people on the telephone. She could imagine what they were like.

'Pleased to meet you over the phone, Dr Hawke,' she said. 'We weren't expecting you for a couple of days.'

'Well, David Miller said to drop in just to have a look round. So I did—and I've ended up working.'

'With Brian Hughes.' She thought for a moment. David Miller, their consultant, was an endocrinologist, with a special interest in paediatric diabetes. They saw patients from all over the North. Brian Hughes was one of them. She went on, 'He has come in with a relapse and a very concerned mother who has assured you that she personally sees to his diet and his medication so it must be his medication at fault and perhaps he ought to have a few days in hospital to sort things out.'

'I see.' The voice at the other end of the line was thoughtful. 'I wish I could diagnose at long distance like that.'

There was no reproof in the voice—in fact, he sounded amused. She felt slightly guilty. 'I'm sorry, Doctor, and I suppose I could be completely wrong, but this will be the fourth time this has happened and Brian has had to come into hospital. And each time it happens when Mrs Hughes has fallen in love again.'

She knew she sounded bitter but she felt no need to conceal it. 'Brian's a lovely kid and he'll be stabilised in a few days. On past form that's about as long as Mrs Hughes's love affair will last.'

'Treat the family not the child,' she heard him murmur. 'Easier said than done. What you say makes sense, Sister McLeod, but I must confess I was completely taken in by his mother. She seemed very worried, very sincere.'

'And very well made-up and very well dressed for a woman beside herself with worry,' Laura said cheerfully. 'Tell me, Doctor, are you reasonably young and attractive?'

She could hear the laughter in his reply. 'You know, Sister, I really couldn't possibly comment on that. Why do you ask?'

'If you are then Mrs Hughes has sat very close to you, held your right forearm and pulled you towards her and explained how difficult it is for a deserted mother to cope. But there is a lot of love inside her and she feels she's one of the world's givers.'

'That's unbelievable! You've got each word, each gesture, right!'

'I've seen it all before. It's a well-rehearsed performance, Dr Hawke.'

'That's sad for the boy. But you're a cynic, Sister.'

'Nothing so destructive. I'm a realist. I hope for the best in people but I don't expect it.'

'I see. Sister McLeod, you've been really helpful. More than that, it's been a real pleasure, talking to you. I look forward to meeting you on the ward. I'm sure we'll get on.'

There was a signal in the warmth of his reply that made her slightly wary. It had happened before. She tended to get too friendly on the telephone. The new S.R. must see her as a nurse, not a woman.

'It's in our patients' best interests if medical and nursing staff co-operate to the full,' she said coolly. 'Now, if you'll excuse me, I really must catch up on my sleep.'

He had noticed her change of tone and was obviously curious as to what he'd said wrong. 'Of course, Sister. And I do apologise for disturbing you when you're off duty.' He rang off.

Laura didn't go to sleep at once. Her gaze wandered

contentedly round the little room she inhabited on the top floor of the nurses' home.

It was plain but the pastel wall colour and beech furniture made it seem quite elegant. She had added her own touches—the shelves full of books, the stack of CDs, the tiny television. There was her tartan bed cover, her prints of Impressionist pictures. On the desk was a narrow cut-glass vase, and she bought herself a single flower once a week. From the window she could see the great trees in the park next to the hospital.

Her life was on the ward, but she could retreat here and be happy. She was self-contained. She didn't really need anyone else.

Seddon General Hospital had its own swimming pool. It was unusual for a hospital, but various departments— Orthopaedics, Midwifery, Paediatrics—had said how valuable the pool was to their work. Mark Black, the chief executive, had fought for the funding.

Laura never had any trouble getting up. If you stayed in bed you tended to half dream, and the world of the imagination could mix with the real world. That was something she didn't want. At half past five next morning her alarm trilled, and before it could stop she was out of bed. Her morning was planned—costume, tracksuit, trainers and towel stood ready. She walked over to the pool.

The attendant smiled at one of the very few who were early morning regulars. In her black one-piece Laura dived in and began her usual steady churn up and down the pool. Two others were doing the same. Laura felt at peace. She loved this quiet time.

Later the pool would fill with people, shouting and splashing. Now was the time for serious swimming. It exercised Laura, and made her relax. She didn't push herself too hard—she wanted to think.

David Miller, the paediatric consultant, had called a ward meeting for later that day. She would meet his new specialist registrar. Laura felt curious about him. He would have to fit in with what was a good, tight-knit team. Usually she was wary of new doctors, but she felt she'd be able to work with this man. She was judging him by his voice—it was gentle, and had made her feel that he was genuinely interested in her as a person. It was a warm voice… Laura told herself to stop dreaming and not be stupid. A gentle voice was a useful tool for a paediatrician, nothing more. She swam the next two lengths at a totally unnecessary speed.

Laura finished her lengths, pulled her tracksuit on over her roughly dried body, and scampered back to her room. There she showered, set her hair in a French plait and put on her uniform.

It was really only half a uniform—a bright tabard over linen trousers and shirt. It was thought that children might be frightened by the stark blue or white worn by nurses in adult wards. Laura recognised this, but still felt sad. A uniform stated who she was, asserted her authority, recorded her achievements.

Quickly she scanned herself in the mirror. Sister McLeod was smart as usual. Her interest was solely in her uniform; the long legs, the slim, firm body didn't concern her. Neither did the high-cheekboned face, the large brown eyes, the softly curved mouth. She knew men found her attractive, but it didn't interest her at present. She was now a nurse, not a woman.

Laura got on well with her opposite number, Ellen Bates, the night sister on Robin Ward. They sat together in the little office and reviewed what had happened during the night. Laura noted that there were two new admissions. Brian Hughes she already knew about, but there was another—Eileen Townley, a five-year-old girl who had been admitted from Casualty the previous night with a gash on the inside of her thigh which had needed thirteen stitches. It had been dangerously near the artery. Laura looked at Ellen questioningly.

'Apparently, it was cut when she fell on an empty bottle,' Ellen said, using the deliberate non-judgemental tone that so many nurses practised. 'A whisky bottle. The parents were having a party. The mother will be in some time this morning—if she can manage it.'

'I'll look forward to seeing her. And Brian Hughes?'

Eileen shrugged. 'She says she's been checking his blood sugar regularly but she can't give us any kind of written proof. He was near hypo. when she brought him in. She swears she's kept him to his diet. I'd say she hasn't. Perhaps she deliberately misfeeds him so he'll have to come into hospital—I just can't tell.'

Laura sighed. A mercifully small number of parents managed to manipulate their children's illnesses, arranging hospital stays as if the hospital were a hotel. She thought Brian's mother was one. 'I'll go and have a word with him when I've finished my book work,' she said.

The other three children in the little four-bedded annexe were down at the day room, but Brian was still in bed. A white face turned to her as she entered, and then there was a cautious smile.

Laura beamed at him. 'Hello, Brian, it's Larry. Remember me? How are you feeling today?'

Brian considered the question carefully. 'Bit better, I think,' he said. 'Still feel tired all the time.'

'Well, we'll see if we can do something about that. Did you stick to your diet, like we told you?'

There was another pause. 'I thought I did. My mam does it mostly and I was getting better. And then I got worse.' Stoically he went on, 'It's rotten, being ill this week. My Uncle Toby's got a boat on the river and we were going on a trip with him. There's a cabin and you can sleep in it. Now my mam will go on her own.'

'I don't think I've met your Uncle Toby,' Laura said delicately.

'He's a new uncle. He's bought me lots of toys.'

'So, do you like him? You get on well together?'

'I suppose he's all right,' Brian said doubtfully. 'He spends a lot of time with my mam. They go out a lot.'

'Well, perhaps you'll get a boat trip some other time. I hope so. Now, sit up a bit and let's have a look at you.' To herself Laura cursed Brian's mother. How could she be so heartless? But she still smiled encouragingly, knowing it would do Brian no good at all to guess what she was thinking. She wondered if the new S.R. would think she was a cynic when he was faced with Brian's case.

Tomorrow was a theatre day and five children were to have tonsillectomies. They were coming in today and she saw the first little party appear at the top of the ward. There was an apprehensive-looking seven-year-old and, if anything, two more apprehensive-looking parents.

She walked down to meet them, her hand outstretched. 'Hello, I'm Sister McLeod and this must be young Harry.' The lad gave an uncertain smile.

'Come and look in the play bay, Harry, and we'll have a talk in a few minutes.'

It was all-important to get to know her young patients as quickly as possible, then she could explain what was going to happen. There might be discomfort and pain, but if the child felt confident things should go well. But five new cases in a day was rather a lot.

Later that morning David Miller, the consultant, held his ward meeting in the sister's office. He believed in keeping the staff informed as much as possible. He said it was the only way to work as a team. Now as many staff as could be spared were squashed together, listening to him and being given the chance to speak if they wished.

'And I'm not very happy about little Peter Ellis's injuries,' he was saying. 'Certainly, they could be the result of a fall, but Peter's had too many falls recently.'

'His mother seems very concerned,' one of the junior nurses said uncertainly. 'I found her crying by his bed. In fact, Peter was quite cheerful until she started him off.'

'I see,' said David thoughtfully. 'She's a quiet girl. Doesn't have much to say for herself. Well, just keep an eye on him. And if you see anything you find peculiar, tell me or Larry here.'

'And remember these are only suspicions,' Laura said firmly. 'We've been wrong about abuse before so don't say anything, especially to the family.'

As she spoke she felt a momentary draught on her neck, indicating that someone had silently opened the door and slipped in. Probably one of the junior nurses. It was only when she registered the unusual interest shown by the staff in front of her that she thought she might be wrong.

She turned. The man behind her must be the new Dr John Hawke. She wasn't sure she liked him.

He was tall and broad-shouldered, and there was an

air of fitness about him. She had doubts about tough, overtly masculine men.

Then he smiled and spoke and she changed her mind a little. His voice *was* attractive, even more so than on the telephone. His smile was gentle. 'Sorry to be late,' he said. 'Quite simply…I got lost.'

There was a ripple of laughter at this confession and David stood to make introductions. 'John Hawke, my new specialist registrar,' he said. 'He's come to us in the northern provinces from London so we'll have to make him welcome. John, this is…'

The meeting was over. Carefully the consultant introduced John to the others in the room, and then they left. Laura noticed that John made a point of speaking to everyone, a slightly longer conversation than was absolutely necessary. He's making a good impression, she thought to herself, and wondered whether it was a coldly chosen technique or a sign of the man's true character. Then she felt ashamed at having thought such a thing.

When it was her turn she found herself looking up into large brown eyes—brown like her own.

'Sister and I have already met,' John said, 'briefly but pleasantly by telephone.'

'Pleased to meet you, Dr Hawke,' Laura said formally. 'I hope you'll enjoy working with us.'

'I'm sure I shall. Now, do I address you as Larry or Laura?'

The question rather threw her. She'd expected him to call her Sister at first. Her half-brothers called her Larry and somehow the name had stuck in her nursing career. But she'd never been too keen on it. 'I'll answer to either,' she said uncomfortably.

'Then I'll call you Laura. It's a beautiful name.'

She blinked. This was a sister's room on a ward. She

didn't expect to hear people talking about what was beautiful.

'I'll leave you in Sister's more than capable hands,' David said. 'Larry, can you show him round? I'd specially like him to look at young Peter.' Then he was gone, and Laura was alone with John Hawke.

Her eyes flicked upwards—he was considerably taller than her own quite respectable five feet six inches. He promptly sat. This intrigued her. He'd realised that she saw his height as a threat, and had tried to do something about it. It showed unusual sensitivity. Most big macho men she knew enjoyed flaunting their size.

She herself sat and said, 'It must be quite an ordeal for you—so many new faces to put names to.'

He didn't reply at once, but thought about it. Then he said, 'New job, new patients, new colleagues…perhaps new friends. There's a lot to get to know. I hope you'll forgive me if I forget something.'

She thought it had been well put. 'I'm sure you'll not forget anything important,' she said. As soon as she'd said it she realised she'd meant it. He seemed relaxed, casual, comforting, but there was a spark of alertness in his eyes. She looked at him a little more closely.

Under his white coat he wore cords and a dark brown woollen shirt with a lighter tie. Paediatric doctors had to tread a difficult path with their clothes. If they were too formal their young charges would be over-awed and not talk. If the dress was too informal parents would get the wrong message. She thought John had it just about right.

She was spending too much time thinking about him! She turned to business. Trying to be efficient, she said, 'If you can just give me a minute I'll sort out the notes for the cases Dr Miller wants you to look at.'

'Whenever you're ready, Laura,' he said, and leaned

back in his chair, perfectly relaxed. She stole a glance and saw that his eyes were shut. Like all doctors, he was adept at cat-napping so she looked more frankly. He had the most gorgeous eyelashes. What a thought!

She saw that his body was lean, rather than heavily muscled. His dark hair was cut a little longer than was usual and curled on his collar. She liked that. She hated the current male fashion for brutally short hair.

At first his face appeared nondescript, apart from the large eyes and gentle, friendly smile. Then she noticed that his mouth was well curved, and she remembered that when he smiled his teeth were good.

'I remember what you said yesterday, Laura.'

With a shock she realised that his eyes had opened and he was talking to her. In dismay at being caught staring at him, she dropped a folder, and bent to scrabble its contents together again. 'Sorry,' she mumbled, red-faced, 'what did I say yesterday?'

'About a doctor-nurse partnership. I agree with you.'

He had caught her staring at him, but there was no knowing smile on his face, no pleasure in her embarrassment. He went on, 'And I'm very much looking forward to working with you.'

'Thank you, Dr Hawke.'

'If I'm to call you Laura then you'll have to call me John.' He grinned mischievously. 'And I don't answer to Johnny.'

He was very easy to talk to. 'Where were you before you came here?' Laura asked curiously.

'I spent five years in St Hilda's in London.'

'It's got a good name. Why did you move here?' She wondered if she'd struck a nerve. For a moment he appeared to frown, as if an unhappy memory had just surfaced.

He shrugged. 'St Hilda's good name is deserved, but I felt I needed a change of scenery and I very much wanted to work with David. So here I am, and looking forward to it. I've...got rid of my London flat and bought one here that is more roomy and much cheaper. So far I'm very happy.'

'Are you...on your own?' she probed delicately.

'Do you mean, am I married? No. Nor do I have what is often euphemistically called a partner.'

Once again Laura felt that she had perhaps trespassed on forbidden territory. There was the slightest touch of bitterness in his voice. She felt her face becoming warm. 'It's just that...we are a team,' she muttered. 'We see each other socially quite a lot. I know the husbands of the other girls and I know David's wife well. We'd just like to make you welcome.'

I'm babbling, she realised.

John's tranquil smile didn't alter. 'I know what hospitals are like and I'm looking forward in time to meeting you all. But I'm afraid I can't contribute a lady. Not at present.'

'You might find one here,' she said, then winced at her own boldness. 'Sorry, I shouldn't have said that. It's not my business, not at all.'

'All things are possible,' he said urbanely.

Hurriedly she offered him the case notes. Why had she said such a thing? It was most unlike her. She had always tired to avoid the semi-flirtatious conversations that she had heard her friends conduct so skilfully. What she wanted was a pleasant, professional relationship based on mutual respect. But she was beginning to know and like this man. He had a non-threatening quality about him. She guessed that he'd be good with children.

A nurse peeped round the door. 'Sister, Mrs Bell wonders if you can spare a minute to talk about her daughter?' John gave her a wave, and left. Laura sighed and switched on her welcoming smile.

She knew that some parents of ill children desperately needed someone to talk to. Partly they needed reassurance—was it their fault that a child had fallen ill? Partly they needed just to go over what had happened, as if repeating the story would make it more believable, more understandable.

Mrs Bell's fourteen-year-old daughter, Vanessa, had been admitted to the ward five days ago. Her GP had recognised diabetes mellitus the minute he'd been called to her bedside. Vanessa was making good progress, but Mrs Bell didn't know where she had gone wrong.

She came into the office and sat, a small neat figure, nervously snapping the catch of her handbag, and told Laura what had happened yet again.

'We thought she was just having an awkward time—girls that age do. She's always been a bit on the plump side so we were really pleased when she started to lose weight. We thought she was slimming. But every time we saw her she was drinking Coke or eating—cakes and things, just what we'd said was bad for her. And she was always going to the loo, sometimes two or three times in the middle of the night. Her teacher phoned and said she didn't seem very well and she had some time off school. Then her breath started to smell like nail-varnish remover—that's when I phoned the doctor.'

Laura sighed. It wasn't an uncommon story.

Mrs Bell went on, 'We've always looked after her and she's always been fit before. Why should this happen to her?'

It was a question a lot of people asked. 'It just happens, I'm afraid,' Laura said, 'but when she's stabilised things won't be so bad. She can still lead a full life.'

'But she'll have to go on a diet! And have injections every day! Can't she take pills or something?'

That too, was what everybody asked. Laura explained that the juices in the stomach would digest the insulin before it could work.

Mrs Bell had heard all this before. David Miller had spent time with her, patiently explaining everything he could, but it was too much to take in at once. Laura knew it would take time before Mrs Bell could live with her daughter's condition. But she'd come round. Most parents did. After a while Mrs Bell went back to her daughter's bedside, perhaps a little less dejected.

The work on the ward was never-ending—as on all wards—but it kept Laura busy and on top of things. There were the children's quarrels to sort out and the occasional attack of home-sickness. There were more parents, bringing in their children for tonsillectomies. Each child had to be made to feel welcome and at ease. It was work she enjoyed.

Then late that morning there was a tap on her door and in came a smartly dressed woman with a tight blonde hairstyle and the longest, reddest nails Laura had ever seen. Mrs Hughes. Laura realised that not all nursing work was pleasant.

'Sorry, Sister,' said Mrs Hughes, preparing to edge away, 'I was looking for Dr Hawke.'

'Come in, Mrs Hughes,' Laura said. 'Have a seat for a moment. Why did you want to see Dr Hawke?'

Mrs Hughes adopted an expression intended to convey motherly care. 'Well, I wanted to ask him about little Brian.'

'I'll tell you about Brian. There's nothing wrong with

him. If he sticks to the diet we've given him and avoids exertion he'll be fine. He'll be out soon.'

That didn't suit Mrs Hughes. 'Oh, no. He's not well enough to—'

'Did you enjoy your trip on the river? With Uncle Toby?' Laura asked. 'Brian was so looking forward to it.'

Mrs Hughes had the grace to blush. 'We couldn't go,' she said. 'Something wrong with the engine. That's why I—'

'Came in to see Brian,' Laura finished off for her. 'Well, I'm sure the three of you will be able to enjoy your trip next week or some time. Now, you can visit Brian and when you come in tomorrow the doctor will be able to tell you when he can go home.'

'I think a longer stay might—' Mrs Hughes started, but Laura cut her off.

'We need the bed,' she said. 'Good afternoon, Mrs Hughes.' Mrs Hughes gave up the struggle and left.

For a moment Laura sat, fighting her ill temper. Mrs Hughes was a single parent with an ill child. Perhaps she needed time to herself. But Laura knew that in similar circumstances most mothers would not be out on the boat with Uncle Toby.

There was a cough behind her and she swung round in her chair to see John. 'I don't usually eavesdrop,' he said, 'but I heard you dealing with Mrs Hughes.'

'It doesn't matter,' Laura said shortly. 'I meant everything I said.'

After a pause he went on. 'You handled that woman very well. You didn't lose your temper but she knew how you felt. You look sweet, but there's steel underneath, isn't there?'

'I'm not sure I want to look sweet,' she said, 'but I'll take it as a compliment.'

Then she felt ashamed as he smiled and said, 'I meant it as a compliment.'

Seddon General Hospital had been built on the site of an old house, Seddon Hall. The rest of the grounds had been turned into a park. Laura took great delight in walking through it. There were long avenues of trees, formal gardens, areas of nothing but grass. She could be out of sight of the hospital in minutes, and believe she was in the heart of the country.

It was Saturday, her rest day, and she'd promised herself a long walk. Autumn was now well established and she thought she liked the reds and golds of the foliage almost as much as the fresh green of spring. It felt good just to walk, with nothing to bother her.

Ahead of her the wind had pushed the fallen leaves into a long pile in the middle of the path. There was no one around so, obeying a childish whim, she ran through the leaves, kicking and dragging her feet, enjoying the dry rustle they made as they moved. It was like paddling, without getting wet, she thought.

'I used to do that when I was younger. Fun, isn't it?'

Laura froze, and wondered why her heart beat just a touch faster. Probably because her solitude had been disturbed, she decided. She had recognised the voice at once. John Hawke's deep, friendly tones were unmistakable.

She turned to see him on the bank above the path. 'What are you doing here?' she asked ungraciously. 'Did you follow me?'

He jumped down easily to join her. 'No, I didn't follow you. My flat's on the other side of the park and I walk through here every day. I like to think of this as my back garden.' As ever, his reply was calming, un-combative, spoken with a little smile.

'It's nice here, isn't it?' she offered. 'I walk here a lot.'

'Much better than London. May I walk with you a while?'

'Of course.' It was courteous of him to ask, she thought as he fell in beside her.

They came to another pile of leaves, and this time it was he who dashed through them, kicking like a seven-year-old. 'Very satisfying,' he said, and she had to giggle.

For a while they walked together in amiable silence. She had noticed this in him before. He knew how and when to keep quiet. It was a capacity not many hard-pressed doctors possessed.

It seemed that he wasn't working today. He was dressed in dark jeans and a navy polo-necked sweater. She thought he looked well in the outfit, broad-shouldered and yet with a trim waist. It was remarkable that she got on with him so well—his kind of macho physique was something that normally she didn't care for. She decided that it was because of the air of serenity he gave out.

'You missed something interesting on the ward yesterday,' she said after a while. 'We had a child in who—'

He put his hand on her shoulder to stop her, and squeezed gently. She was almost surprised at the tingle his gesture gave her. 'No, Laura,' he said. 'That ward has filled your life for the past six days. I've watched you at work. It's filled mine, too. I was awake till two this morning, reading up on some recent American research on childhood diabetes. Now we've got a few minutes away from the hospital it'll do us good to talk about something else.'

She felt a faint sense of unease. She liked talking about work—it was unprovocative. Still, she realised that what he'd said was true. 'What d'you want to talk about?' she asked. She couldn't think of anything herself.

'Well…tell me about this park.'

Good, that was safe. She rattled on about Lord Seddon, giving the park to the town on condition that the grounds were kept up to a high standard and that there were security patrols day and night. 'I've always felt safe here,' she explained.

'Always? So you're a local girl?'

'Yes. I went to the local grammar school. All I ever wanted to be was a nurse so I trained here and I've been here ever since.'

'So, do you have a family nearby? I thought you lived in the nurses' home.'

'I have quite a big family,' she said carefully, 'and I see them as often as I can, but I prefer to live next door to my work. All my friends are in the hospital so it's very handy.'

'I see. It looks a comfortable nurses' home. Much better than the ones on London.' She had learned that it was typical of the man that he didn't press her. He had recognised that there was something she didn't want to discuss and respected her wishes.

They walked on further. The path climbed out of its little alley and they could see the expensive houses that lined the park. The next question, when it came, was couched gently. 'Are you in any special relationship yourself, Laura? Do tell me to mind my own business if you want.'

For some reason she didn't mind telling him. 'No, there's no special man in my life. There have been and I have some men friends, of course, but...' She waved a hand to indicate they were of little importance.

Surprisingly she felt the urge to say more, to justify herself. 'I've nothing against men. It's just that I have so little time. My work is all-important to me.'

'I know,' he said drily. 'I've seen you doing it.'

By now they were near the edge of the park. John pointed to a small block of flats. 'That's where I live. The top floor flat on the right—with the new plant pots on the balcony.'

She looked. It was a modern block in a well-appointed garden. Just for once she wondered what it would be like to have a home of her own, something that was really hers. She was happy in the nurses' home but she knew she was really only a tenant.

'It looks very smart,' she said. 'You've got a lovely view.'

'Would you like to come in for a coffee? I've just bought some Jamaica Blue Mountain.'

She was tempted but she knew she shouldn't. 'I'd love to but, no, thanks. I've got to get back and—'

'Wash your hair?' He grinned.

It was said with complete absence of malice, and she had to laugh. 'Nearly, but not quite. I have to wash my clothes, not my hair.'

'I see. Well...even better, would you like to come and have a drink with me tonight? We could go to the Seddon Arms. It's quite pleasant there. And they serve excellent suppers.'

From him it was a gentle, unthreatening invitation.

Once again she was tempted, but she knew that, for her, invitations like that were better refused. 'It's very kind of you,' she said, 'but I don't think so. We have to work together and it could lead to…complications. But I know half a dozen other nurses who'd love to have a drink with you. We're all agreed on one thing. You're a definite improvement on Dr Chan, the man you replaced.'

He smiled. 'Well, that is reassuring. But I don't want just a drink with a nurse—though I like them all. I want a drink with you. Still, you've made up your mind. Will you be all right, walking back through the park on your own?'

'Yes…yes,' Laura said uncertainly. 'Perfectly all right.'

'Good afternoon, then, Laura.' He touched her once on the shoulder, turned and walked away. She watched as he reached the park wall, and lithely vaulted over. She turned away. Had she done the right thing? Would she be wary all her life? Sometimes she thought she was too hard on herself.

CHAPTER TWO

THE next day was unusually warm, one of those rare autumn days that harked back to high summer. It was so fine that Laura couldn't get on with the little household duties that seemed to build up in the week, and she decided she'd walk in the park again.

The unseasonable weather had brought out crowds, and even an ice-cream van. She idled past the playground, listening to the shrieks from children on the slides and swings. With approval she noted that the old concrete had been resurfaced with a special rubber-based compound. She'd lost count of the number of children who had come into Casualty with cuts and bruises because of that rough surface!

'Is bad boy, Timmy! Come back to Helga!'

'Won't! I'm an engine!'

Laura smiled secretly at the family scene, being played on one of the grassy slopes. A little boy of about six was rushing up the bank and rolling down again. He was thoroughly enjoying himself. His guardian, a harassed-looking girl in her twenties, was trying in vain to keep him in order. There was something about her clothes that suggested she wasn't English.

'You should not run—come here,' she called.

Laura thought it was a bit unnecessary. There were no motor vehicles allowed in the park and the boy was quite safe.

Anyway, he paid no attention. 'Shan't,' he shouted. I

wouldn't have that if he was on my ward, Laura thought
to herself.

Since it was so warm she bought herself an ice cream.
Vaguely she wondered if she'd seen the little boy before.
His face seemed familiar. No matter, she saw lots of
children. In town she was always being greeted by half-
remembered patients she'd treated two, three or four
years before. And they'd grown!

She looked at the ducks, enjoyed her ice cream and
wandered aimlessly onwards.

Somehow her steps led her to the same path as yesterday—and before she fully realised it she was standing
opposite John's flat. There was his balcony with the new
planters. It curved round two sides of the building so
that there'd be maximum sun. A figure flitted across the
glass behind the balcony, and she turned abruptly. She
shouldn't be so silly. So far she liked John, but she still
didn't know him very well. She was wary of men. She'd
have to know him better before she'd…before she'd
what?

She walked towards the hospital, her pace faster now
and more determined. She passed the foreign girl, sitting
on her coat. The little boy's exertions must have worn
him out. He was asleep with his head on the girl's leg,
her arm protectively round him.

Laura strode on. Then her steps slowed and her forehead creased as she tried to dig something out of the
back of her memory. For some reason something was
irritating her subconscious. That little boy…Timmy?
Had she nursed a Timmy? She'd got it! Timmy Roscoe!

She hadn't nursed him herself, but she remembered
the mother. Mrs Roscoe was tall and well dressed, with
the overbearing manner of some wealthy people. When
she got excited her voice betrayed her—she'd not been

born to money. Laura remembered her speaking to a nurse who was desperately trying to remain polite.

'Of course, we could have gone privately but my husband insisted we use the public health service. I don't know why.'

This was all irrelevant—what was her subconscious trying to tell her? Then she remembered. Timmy was a diabetic. He'd come into hospital to be diagnosed and stabilised, and had been sent home with the customary list of instructions.

Surely Mrs Roscoe would have warned this foreign girl about Timmy's state? Exercise—exertion—was fine but it had to be monitored and the correct level of insulin maintained, otherwise there was the danger of low blood sugar—hypoglycaemia. Children were far more easily affected and far more quickly affected than adults. Probably Timmy was just having a sleep. But what if he were in a hypoglycaemic coma?

Laura was torn. She was not on her ward now—not in the uniform which gave her dignity and authority. She also remembered what one of her tutors had told her while she was training. 'You'll see people doing stupid, health-endangering things. Smoking is one. It's not your place to interfere or offer advice unless it's asked for. You'll usually get rebuffed.'

She walked on another dozen steps, then turned. She had to go back. The young woman looked up warily as Laura approached, and her arm tightened round Timmy. She didn't respond to Laura's smile. 'Hello, Timmy,' Laura said hopefully, even though the boy was obviously asleep. To the young woman Laura said, 'I used to nurse him. At the hospital over there.'

'He is asleep,' the girl answered. 'Very tired. Please not interfere. Go away.'

Closer to Timmy now, Laura didn't want to go away. His lips were unusually red, there were beads of perspiration on his forehead and he looked pale—paler than when she'd seen him a few minutes ago.

'What is your name?' Laura asked. 'Helga,' the girl replied.

Carefully Laura said, 'I'm a nurse, Helga, and I remember Timmy. He's diabetic, isn't he? Can I get him a drink or something—a Coke perhaps? Then we could walk over to the hospital and—'

She was quite unprepared for Helga's reaction. 'Go away!' the girl screamed. 'You are trying to steal my baby. Mrs Roscoe said are people like you. They say from hospital and they offer drinks!'

'Are you all right, love?' a voice asked from behind Laura. 'Is this woman troubling you?'

'She is the woman in the paper. She steals babies and offers drinks of Coke. Now she is trying to take Timmy!' Both Helga's arms were now wrapped round Timmy and she crushed him to her. Even in the middle of this nightmare Laura's trained eye noticed that Timmy didn't move or struggle. And he should have done.

'Look,' Laura said desperately, 'I'm a nurse and I work over there in the hospital and—'

'That's what the other one said. The paper said she'd probably try to steal another baby. We'll get the police on you!' Someone behind Laura gave her a push, and she stumbled forward onto her hands and knees. This couldn't be happening to her!

Suddenly she understood what was wrong. The previous week a young woman dressed in nursing uniform had tried to take a child from a nursing home on the other side of town. She'd asked the mother if she could buy the child a Coke, and the mother had caught her, trying to drag her daughter into a car. So far the police hadn't been successful in catching the woman.

There was now a crowd gathered round, half solicitous for Helga and Timmy, half angry at Laura. Someone had grasped Laura painfully by the arm and no one was paying any attention to her protestations of innocence.

'I'm a nurse,' she cried. 'I tell you I—'

'Never mind the police! Let's deal with her ourselves. She'll only get let off.' This time it was a fat woman speaking, her face contorted with rage. It seemed inconceivable that a crowd could gather so quickly, could get so ugly and be so wrong. Laura was terrified. And no one was listening to her!

'Let me through now! I'm a doctor. And get back from that child.'

She thought they were the sweetest words she'd ever heard. She recognised the voice, if not the tone. It was John Hawke, speaking in a rasping, authoritative voice that silenced the crowd immediately.

'Take your hand off that girl's arm.' She felt herself released. It was usually easy to see exactly what John was feeling. Now the crowd saw the anger in his face and did exactly what he said.

'Are you all right, Laura?'

She nodded, then pointed to Timmy. 'He was in Sparrow Ward a while ago. I saw him running earlier—I think he might have gone hypo. This must be his nanny—Helga. She thought I was trying to steal the child.'

With a touch of annoyance she noticed that Helga didn't object at all when John felt Timmy's forehead and stomach and gently took him.

'Help me put him in the recovery position, will you,

Nurse?' John asked quietly, and she helped him ease Timmy onto his side so that if he vomited he wouldn't choke. Then, as best he could, John carried on with his examination.

'Is there anything we can do, Doctor?' It was the man who had grabbed her so painfully by the arm, now apparently quite happy to change sides. People! Laura thought. Why can't they think before they act?

'Go over to that café and ask for a spoonful of sugar.' John turned to Helga, who now looked decidedly tearful. Gently he asked, 'Did you have any instructions about Timmy, Helga?'

The girl produced a small plastic carrier. 'There is Coke to drink here and I am not to let him run too far. But he's a bad boy! He does not do as I say.'

'Is there any problem here?' Another person had joined the crowd of eager spectators but this one was more welcome, dressed in the blue uniform of the park police.

John looked up. 'I'm a doctor. Nurse here and myself think this child has gone into a hypoglycaemic coma. Certainly he needs hospital attention. Have you got a vehicle here?'

'Yes, sir. I'll phone my partner to drive it up.'

'Fine. Now, if you could just get this crowd to step back a little?'

'Here's your sugar.' A panting man returned and handed John a screwed-up napkin. John opened it, dipped his finger into the white granules and with his other hand gently pried open Timmy's mouth.

'Not the most sterile of procedures, Laura,' he muttered, then rubbed the sugar on the inside of Timmy's cheek.

Both waited hopefully. The speed with which a hypoglycaemic child could return to normality was one of the most heart-warming sights in paediatric medicine. But not this time. 'Too late for a glucagon injection,' John said. 'He needs a glucose drip. I don't like hypoglycaemic attacks going this far in young children. Let's have him back on Sparrow Ward.'

The crowd parted to let a green-painted Land Rover through. John stood, lifting Timmy easily in his arms. 'Helga, you must come to the hospital with us and we'll phone Timmy's parents from there. Don't worry, none of this was your fault. We'll explain everything there.' They all climbed into the Land Rover and it lurched off the bank. John borrowed the park policeman's radio and phoned Sparrow Ward. Then he smiled at Laura. 'We're in luck. David Miller's on the ward. All we have to do is deposit this little mite and then carry on with our break.'

'It was lucky you turned up,' Laura said. 'I don't think I could have coped. That crowd was getting unreasonable.'

'It wasn't luck. I saw you outside my flat and I thought you might change your mind about coming in for coffee so I came looking for you.'

'Well, it was lucky for Timmy,' she said.

She felt guilty at having been caught, staring at his flat, but was surprisingly pleased at him chasing after her.

They arrived at Sparrow Ward, and a trolley and nurse were already waiting at the door. Timmy was hurried in. John thanked the two park policemen and suggested they ran Helga home. He would phone the parents at once. Then John said, 'See you in a couple of minutes.' He disappeared after Timmy. Suddenly Laura felt a sense of anticlimax.

'What's this, Larry? Picking up patients off the street?' Ann Adams, Sister on Sparrow Ward, bustled up with a smile. Laura felt more lost than ever. Without her uniform she was an interloper here.

'You seem to have everything under control now,' she said, looking down the ward. David and John were in earnest consultation by the side of Timmy's bed.

'We're not too busy,' Ann agreed. 'D'you want to wait in the office till John's finished?'

No, she didn't want that. But she knew she couldn't go home. 'Since I'm here, I'll go into the back room and do a few reports,' she said. 'You don't mind, do you, Ann?'

'Be my guest. Shall I tell Dr Hawke where you are if he asks for you?'

'No. Tell him you think I've gone home. We only met by accident.'

Ann looked at her expressionlessly. 'Whatever you say, dear,' she said.

Behind the sister's room there was another room, a windowless closet really, its shelves piled high with occasionally used equipment. But there was also a table and a chair. Laura sat, facing a blank pad, and sighed. She could catch up on her paperwork.

Sometimes she wondered if she were a clerk or a nurse. There seemed to be more and more paperwork—requisitions, future plans, scheduling, reports on staff and services. She'd discovered early on that the only way to cope was never to put anything off.

'Natalie Platt', she wrote at the top of her paper. Natalie was a Project 2000 student, one of the new breed of training nurses. Instead of starting work on a ward and getting used to the hard side of nursing, Project 2000 nurses began with a long period of book-learning. Laura wasn't sure it was the right way to teach a nurse. Still, they'd have to give the system a chance.

Natalie had come onto the ward, technically to 'observe'—whatever that meant. Now Laura had to write a short report on her. She thought for a moment, then started to write.

Once started, the work flowed well. After ten minutes there was the sound of the outside door opening and an imperious voice said, 'My name is Mrs Roscoe. I've been dragged away from a most important meeting. Apparently my son Timmy is causing trouble again—where is he?'

There was a mutter of calming tones and Laura went back to her work.

Perhaps she should have thought and moved. After another fifteen minutes there was the sound of the door opening and shutting again, the hum of voices and then, just the other side of the flimsy door to the back room, a voice said, 'That stupid girl, Helga. I suppose I ought to dismiss her—but she's so good in so many ways.' Mrs Roscoe, being as unpleasant as she usually was.

John's voice was equally clear. 'Did she know about Timmy's condition, Mrs Roscoe? Did she know about the dangers of over-exertion?'

Mrs Roscoe sniffed. 'What is there to know? All this talk about diabetes being a lifelong condition—it's all rubbish. There's nothing wrong with Timmy.'

With a twitch of discomfort Laura realised what had happened. She was trapped. There was no way she could walk out of the back room now. There was also no way she could avoid hearing everything that was said. She hated the idea of being an eavesdropper, but what could she do?

Mrs Roscoe hadn't stopped. 'I sometimes wonder if

you didn't misdiagnose him. Oh, he's ill now all right, but a few days in hospital and—'

'You were told about the honeymoon period? Where it appears that everything is fine? And that you must not under any circumstances think that your child is cured?'

'Yes. But he seemed so—'

Something had happened to John's voice. Mrs Roscoe didn't appear to have noticed but Laura certainly had. He still spoke slowly, gently, but there was an edge underneath that she'd never heard before. With an odd thrill she discovered that he was capable of much greater passion than she'd thought. Her picture of him as merely a calm, kind, imperturbable doctor was flawed.

John said, 'Mrs Roscoe, you disregarded specific hospital instructions about your child's welfare. Those instructions weren't given to annoy you—they were to ensure that Timmy had as near a normal life as could be expected. In fact, they were to ensure that Timmy had a life at all. By your selfishness, lack of consideration and pure stupidity you put your child's life at risk. We may have to contact Social Services to decide if yours is a suitable home for an ill child. Good afternoon, Mrs Roscoe.' The door closed quietly.

Laura didn't know what to think. This was a side of John she'd never suspected. Such anger! She shivered as she thought what it must be like to be on the receiving end of such cold fury. Not, though, that Mrs Roscoe hadn't deserved every word.

She heard the rattle of a phone. Mrs Roscoe, her voice quaking with anger, snapped, 'I want a line out—now! All right, I'll dial nine first.' There was the sound of dialling and Mrs Roscoe's mutter. 'He can't talk to me like that, I won't have it—Harry!' The voice was now strident. 'Yes, it is important. I'm at the hospital and the

doctor here has just treated me like dirt! I won't stand
for it. I— Well, Timmy had a bit of a relapse... Well,
it could have been but he's all right now... No, in the
park with Helga... Some nurse or doctor found him.
Now, I want that doctor disciplined. I—Harry...*Harry*!'

The door was slammed, quite unnecessarily, and there
was the clatter of shoes down the corridor. Laura sighed
with relief. She remembered the old hospital axiom.
Every child means at least two patients—the child and
its mother. She was glad she didn't have to deal with
Mrs Roscoe, though she knew she could if she had to.

All this was too wearing. Clutching her pad of notes,
she peered warily out of her hiding place, then scampered off to the safety of her own little room.

She was on lates the next day. When she had a minute
she popped over from Robin to Sparrow Ward for a
quick word about Timmy. As she scanned his notes she
first shuddered, and then a vague feeling of professional
pride crept over her. She had been right to interfere. A
hypoglycaemic attack in a young child could be serious.
Yes, she'd been right.

There was an extra small job on her ward, involving
the children who had had tonsillectomies the day before.
They had to eat something that would scrape the tonsil
bed, cleaning it of dried blood or little scabs. Crisps or
cornflakes or toast would do. It was undeniably painful
but it had to be done to stop the tonsils from becoming
infected. Some children suffered stoically, some made a
fuss. The worst this time was a fifteen-year-old boy, who
was about six inches taller than Laura. The only way she
managed to get him to eat a very small piece of toast
was to shame him—showing him an eight-year-old girl

who silently ate what she was given while the tears ran down her face.

So work continued on Robin, sometimes easy, sometimes hard, always fascinating. At five she sat in her room for a coffee and a chocolate biscuit, needing the energy.

There was a knock on the door and a head looked round it. 'Sister McLeod? May I have a word? My name's Harry Roscoe.'

'Come in, Mr Roscoe. Would you like a coffee?'

She liked him. He was a short, broad man with bright, shrewd blue eyes and a cheerful local accent. His suit was obviously expensive but he managed to wear it as if he didn't care. He sat in the chair offered and accepted a mug of coffee. All the time he looked at her, curiously but not unpleasantly.

'You saved Timmy's life yesterday,' he said abruptly.

Laura shook her head. 'No. If anyone did it was Dr Hawke.'

'I've spoken to him and thanked him. But you spotted Timmy's condition first. Helga would have taken him back home and left him in bed for the rest of the day. If you hadn't stuck your neck out and interfered, he could now be dead. That's true, isn't it?'

As he looked at her Laura had the odd feeling that she was being submitted to some kind of test. But basically he was right. Cautiously she said, 'Timmy certainly could have been very ill indeed.'

'I've heard about that little scene in the park. But you still stuck to what you knew was right. Now, first of all, thank you. Timmy's my only child—we can't have any more. I think you know what I'm feeling so I'd like to give you something.'

'There is absolutely no—' she started, but he held up his hand.

'Please! I know what you're going to say, but this is my guilt talking. I've spent too much time earning money and not enough looking after my son. I'll change now. And if I give you something it'll be, well, therapy.'

Laura had to laugh at the hopeful expression on his face. 'I hope all therapy isn't so expensive. I'll tell you what. I don't need anything—I'm reasonably well paid—but if you'd like to buy a couple of toys for the ward, I'd be delighted and you'd bring joy to a lot of children.'

'Done.' From inside his jacket pocket he took a cheque book, wrote busily for a few moments on the back and front then offered the slip of paper to Laura. 'Here. Do what you want with this. I'm going back to sit with Timmy. And, Sister—thanks again.'

He was at the door before she had time to say anything. Then he turned and added, 'Oh, I just heard the news. That poor creature who tried to steal a baby. The police have picked her up. Apparently she's just come out of psychiatric care.'

Laura nodded sadly, then glanced at the cheque as he moved through the door. It was open—for three hundred pounds! 'Thank you, Mr Roscoe,' she muttered faintly.

By nine o'clock that evening things had eased considerably. The younger children were asleep and the older ones were playing computer games or watching television. Laura was concentrating on her troublesome reports again.

'Laura—don't get up.' It was John, now back in his white coat, but this time with a dark blue shirt and tie. She hadn't seen him since the previous day, and was unprepared for the rush of sheer joy his arrival brought her.

'John. Is there anything I—?'

'I'm being fussy. I just want another look at Peter Ellis. No need for you to come on the ward. I'll come back if I need you.' He moved further into her room. 'You look a bit out of sorts. Everything all right?'

She waved the pink cheque at him. 'Timmy's dad's just been in. He's left us a cheque for three hundred pounds to spend on toys. It seems rather a lot of money. Should we spend it all?'

'You must certainly spend the cheque,' John said with some surprise in his voice. 'Harry Roscoe can afford it. He was telling me he's the owner of Roscoe's Travel Shops.'

'I should have guessed,' Laura said thoughtfully. There was a Roscoe Travel Shop in the high street of most of the local towns. They had a reputation for providing a good personal service even if they weren't the cheapest of travel agents.

'So I'm OK for a coffee in about ten minutes?' John asked urbanely.

'I wouldn't want you passing out on my ward. If you say something gloomy about low blood sugar I'll even see if I can run to a garibaldi biscuit.'

'Just checked my blood sugar. It's down to a ludicrously low level. I'm suffering from extreme fatigue, hallucinations, delusions, anxiety attacks and in general I'm a twitching nervous wreck.'

Laura looked at him as he leaned casually against her wall, legs crossed, hands in pockets, amiable half-smile on his face. She'd never seen anyone look less like a nervous wreck.

'Get out of my office,' she said, making shooing

movements with her hands. 'Leave a poor harassed sister to her toil.'

She smiled as she retrieved the tin from its locked bottom drawer. Garibaldi biscuits were an unusual treat. She didn't want her little charges to see her eating them.

A thought struck her. There had been no real need for John to come and see Peter Ellis. He was in for observation, and so far there had been no cause for alarm. His cuts and bruises were improving and it now seemed as if he really had got them through a fall. There was no evidence of abuse. Had John come to see him? Or had he come in what he knew was a quiet time so he could see her?

Since she had a few minutes to spare, she decided to make a cafetièere of specially bought coffee instead of the usual instant. The rich aroma filled her little room, for a while quite defeating the ever-present smells of soap and disinfectant. She put a cloth on a tray, laid out cups and biscuits on a plate and stood back like a proud housewife to survey her little bit of gracious living.

Her phone rang. 'Sister McLeod, Robin Ward,' she answered abstractedly.

'Hi, Larry, it's your hard-drinking Auntie Sal. How's my little girl?'

Laura stood motionless for a moment, her anticipation of a pleasant ten-minute coffee-break with John dashed by her feelings of guilt. Sal Wilmot was her aunt, the woman who had brought her up, the woman who had done all she could to provide a warm and loving home for her younger sister's orphaned child. Laura knew she should visit her more often.

She forced herself to be cheerful. 'Sal, how are you? I bet I know where you're phoning from.' Behind Sal's voice she could hear the hum of conversation, the occasional outburst of raucous laughter, the clink of glasses.

'I'll bet you do, kid. I'm sitting here on my favourite stool at my favourite club.'

Laura could picture it. Sal was at the bar of the Gilmour Rugby Club, a smart club in the prosperous suburb of Gilmour. Sal went there most nights. She'd be sitting with a cigarette in her hand and a double whisky on the bar in front of her. There would be a little group of friends round her—a doctor, a solicitor, people with local businesses. Sal was a smart, shrewd woman who liked good company and found it in the club. Once Laura, too, had been a regular visitor, but now she didn't like it. She couldn't let Sal know. She'd want to know why.

Sal went on, 'We've not heard from you for quite a while. You haven't found a man, have you, honey? A nice rich doctor? Bring him home and let me have a look at him.'

'I'm not looking for a man,' Laura said with some asperity, 'especially a doctor. No, I've just been too busy on the ward. It never stops, Sal.'

'If you work too hard then you get stale. Then your looks suffer. Take it from me, Larry. I've been there.'

'I guess you're right.' Laura sighed. 'I should take things easier.' The trouble was that she agreed with Sal. Her aunt owned three hairdressing salons and was thought to be an efficient and caring manager.

'Anyway, business of the call,' Sal went on. 'Buster's coming home from university next Saturday and he's particularly asked for you. He's playing in the afternoon. Can you come over for the match and stay for the party afterwards? We haven't seen you for quite a while.'

Laura flinched at the gentle reproach in Sal's voice.

'Let me look at my work sheet,' she said. 'I've got it here in my bag. How's Robert getting on?' Laura just couldn't force herself to call her youngest half-brother Buster. He was Robert. He'd always been her favourite of Sal's three sons. Technically they were her cousins, she supposed, but she'd always thought of them as more or less brothers.

There was a touch of sensitivity in Robert. The two older brothers, Clive and Colin, loved Laura, would do anything for her and had as much understanding of her as if they'd been born on Mars.

'He's doing fine,' Sal said. 'Plays regularly for the county and has just had a trial for the English team.'

'How's he doing at university?' Laura asked patiently. 'How are his studies going?'

Sal was dismissive. 'Oh, he'll be all right. You've all done all right at your studies.' That was true. In spite of—or because of—their rugby-playing, both Clive and Colin had done well. Laura supposed she had done well, too.

'I've got my diary here,' she said. 'I'm on lates. I could probably swap an early bit of the shift, but I can't stay for the party.'

'That's a pity, it should be a good do. Are you sure you can't swing the entire shift?'

'It's Saturday night,' Laura pointed out. 'Everyone's out on the town.' She knew Sal would respond to this argument. Sal couldn't imagine anyone not wanting to go out on the weekend.

'That's true. You should have come into the hairdressing business with me, instead of becoming a nurse. Anyway, come to the house in the morning and help me make sandwiches.'

'I'll be there as soon as I can. Look, Sal, I'm wanted. I'll have to go. See you Saturday.'

'Bye, Larry. Love from us all.' The phone was put down.

Love from us all. They all did love her, and she loved them, but she couldn't live their kind of masculine life. It revolved around the rugby club—and that wasn't for her. Well, not now.

'Do I smell coffee?'

It was not a good time for John to come in. 'I'll pour you one,' she said briefly. 'Help yourself to biscuits.'

She caught the troubled flash of appraisal in his eyes. He'd sensed the abrupt change in her mood, even though she'd tried to conceal it. There was a sour atmosphere in the little room, and it was all her fault.

Somehow she had to make amends. He was a good doctor, a pleasant man, and she shouldn't visit her problems on him. Or, worse, have him think she was temperamental, always in a mood. Every hospital knew of nurses like that, and they were no end of trouble.

With some difficulty she said, 'I've just had a phone call from home. Families can cause problems, can't they?'

She had expected him to agree with her and accept her half-explanation, half-apology for her chilly behaviour. Instead, he took her question seriously.

'They can cause problems, certainly, but they don't have to. Think of the mothers of the diabetic children we have here. Only about two per cent don't cope. Perhaps seventy-five per cent do very well. They learn to handle injections, they deal with diet, they keep a keen eye on the child's progress. They do more than manage. We're a doctor and a nurse—injections are nothing to us. But imagine a young mum—and some of them *are* young. She has to stick a needle into her baby. When I see things going so well, and so often, then I'm heartened.'

Laura felt small. He hadn't said it, but what he had suggested was right. Her problems were insignificant. Once again it struck her just how insightful he was. He was more than a good clinical doctor—he had the feel for people that could make him a great one.

They were now sitting on each side of her desk, contentedly sipping coffee. With a slight shock Laura realised that her out-of-sorts feeling had disappeared. John had a calming effect on her, just as he had on children.

He smiled at her, and she knew he was going to ask her about her family so she jumped in first. 'Tell me about your family,' she suggested, and coloured just a little when he shot her a half-humorous glance.

'My family?' She knew he'd interpreted her question as a way to avoid answering questions about her own family. 'Do you really want to know?'

She found that she did. She wanted to know more about him. 'This is most unusual,' she said. 'Just for once I'm not wanted on the ward. So—if you don't mind talking?'

He poured himself another coffee and she thought his open face clouded slightly. She hoped she hadn't upset him. Being a nurse, she knew that not every family story was a happy one.

'My parents worked—still work, in fact—in Africa. They're based on a place called Anwaro—it's hot, unhealthy and dangerous. My dad's an administrator, my mother a nurse.'

'You're an only child?' Laura put in.

He nodded. 'Sadly, yes. I would have liked brothers and sisters. Anyway, it seemed to them that the best thing for me was to put me in a boarding school. I wasn't unhappy there—I was good at sports and bright enough academically—but I envied the other kids. They had parents who came to see them—often.'

'Is that why you decided to specialise in paediatrics?'

'Probably. I like kids. And I saw too many abandoned by rich parents.'

He stopped for a moment and she didn't want to interrupt his train of thought. He seemed to be musing, trying to make sense of what he was saying. 'You know, Laura, here in hospital we only do half of the work with sick kids. Parents can be a nuisance, but it's they who do the important part of curing.'

There was a troubled pause and then he said, 'Don't get me wrong. My parents loved and cared for me—they still do—but because they weren't there when I was young there's a barrier between us. We feel it, we're saddened by it, but we can't break it. Perhaps, if ever I have kids of my own, that'll be the way of getting across to them.'

Laura was fascinated by this. She also felt privileged. John had revealed his soul to her with a candour that was breath-taking.

Slowly she said, 'But you're not married yet—and you want to be. Why not?'

'Don't mind asking personal questions, do you, Sister McLeod?' he said with a grin.

She felt the blood mounting to her cheeks again. 'Sorry,' she said, 'I know it's none of my business.'

'No problem. It's a question I'll answer. One, I've been too busy. Two, I have had relationships—one of them quite—well, very—serious. I thought I loved her but the woman in question couldn't give me what I wanted. She had her own ideas about her future. So we parted, quite amicably, and I'm still looking. I think nothing, by the way, of the idea of trying marriage and then getting divorced if it doesn't work. I'd rather be certain first.'

It was a simple enough story but it gave Laura quite a lot to think about. She felt she knew him better now, and could understand the instant empathy he had with the children. She knew why he gave out an air of calm, of solidarity. She also wanted to know an awful lot more. What couldn't this woman give him? She must have been mad.

With a tiny touch of panic she realised something else. Stories were to be shared. He'd put her under an obligation to tell him her story, and she wasn't quite sure she wanted to.

John reached out and patted her hand. When he spoke she found with a shock that he'd read her thoughts. 'I really would like to know about your life, but you're not to feel that you've got to tell me. If it's going to cause you pain don't worry about it. Honestly.'

'I wish you didn't know what I'm thinking,' she grumbled quietly. 'My life's been quite simple, really. You'll have heard a lot of people call me Larry. That's because—'

'Oh, no, what's Dr Hawke doing here? Don't say there's trouble on the ward?'

Laura looked up. She saw it was Ellen Bates, the night sister, her middle-aged face beaming. She glanced at her watch—where had the last half-hour gone? it was time for change-over.

John stood. 'No trouble, Ellen,' he said. 'I came to look at young Peter Ellis but I'm happy with him now. I just stayed for the best biscuits in the hospital.'

He turned to Laura. 'It's been a long day. I think I'll

go for a quiet drink in the Dragon Bar.' And he was gone.

Ellen looked after him with approval. 'Now, I wish he'd come and see me some quiet time. The very sight of him makes me remember when I was a girl again. You're a lucky person, Laura.'

'Rubbish,' Laura said, pulling a face. 'Pour yourself a coffee, Ellen. I'll just get the notes together.'

She ignored Ellen's knowing smile.

CHAPTER THREE

LAURA nearly didn't go. First she muttered to herself that she wanted to get out of her uniform after a long day. Then she decided she was far too tired to socialise. Then she forced herself to be honest. She wanted to go for a drink with John.

The Dragon Bar was a tiny social club for members of the hospital only. It was in the oldest part of the complex, the section which had once been the stables of the old Seddon Hall. Mark Black, the chief executive, felt that his staff were hard-working and entitled to some small privileges. The Dragon Bar was one. It was comfortable, luxurious even, with thick carpets and low lights. Tables were arranged in odd corners and recesses, with low-slung chairs around them. It was a place to sit with friends and relax.

Outside the door she hesitated again. She wasn't one of the doctors or nurses who needed a drink after each hard session. She'd seen staff get too fond of 'just one drink' every night. But there was this bargain between them, more pressing, she felt, because it had been unspoken. She pushed open the mahogany door and entered.

She saw him straight away. He'd picked a table where he'd be immediately obvious to anyone entering. Another example of his thoughtfulness, she decided. As she approached him he stood, a broad and genuine smile on his face.

'It's so good to see you, Laura,' he said. 'I hinted and

I was hoping you'd come. In fact...' he indicated the table '...I guessed your taste and got you a drink.'

'I can't stay long,' Laura said, and then felt ungracious.

He didn't appear to notice. 'I've work myself tomorrow.' He made sure she was comfortable in her chair, before seating himself. 'The barman assured me that most people find this Saumur really pleasing. In fact—I cannot tell a lie—I had a wee taste and he's right.'

She smiled at his mock contrite expression and then sipped from the tall glass of white wine he pushed towards her. 'It *is* good,' she said. 'What are you drinking?'

He indicated a pint glass. 'I'm trying the local bitter. I didn't believe in the North–South divide until I came here and drank the beer. The Northern brew is much superior.'

She frowned. She didn't much like beer-drinkers.

He offered her a nut from the glass tray between them and then took one himself, his strong white teeth biting with evident enjoyment. 'I want to know why an obviously feminine young lady is called Larry,' he said. 'And I want to know all kinds of other things about you. But if you don't want to talk that's fine.'

It was a generous-minded offer, she decided, and sat in silence for a while to consider it. 'What if there are things in my past I don't want to talk about?' she asked.

'Then by all means don't talk about them. But it's been my experience that a lot of things people keep secret are less frightening when they're talked about.'

Secrets are frightening. Possibly.

She took a mouthful of wine and said, 'The first thing you have to know about me is that I'm illegitimate.' She let the bald statement echo there between them.

After a while he asked gently, 'Am I supposed to comment?'

'If you want to.' She was conscious that her voice was challenging.

'Then I would just say that the idea of a newborn baby doing anything illegitimate is foolish in the extreme. Illegitimate parents are possible—they should have the power to decide on their actions.'

It was a typical John answer, thoughtful and non-argumentative. Laura knew it would make her story easier to tell. 'I know that's true,' she said, 'but sometimes I just don't feel it.'

After a moment's thought she said, 'I loved my mother, but she died when I was five. She had a brain tumour. One minute she was there, the next minute she was in hospital and then...she was dead.'

'You remember her?'

'I have this dim memory of her. A memory of calm, peace and protection.'

'And then?' His question led rather than pushed her.

'I was brought up by my mother's older sister—Auntie Sal. I tried to call her Auntie but she said she wanted to be called Sal. She was divorced, had three boys, two older than me, and ran—still runs—a set of hairdressing salons. She never hesitated. They all took me in. That was when I started to be called Larry.'

'They treated you as an extra boy?'

She gave him a small smile. 'They loved me, and did all they could to look after me. We were just one big boisterous family.'

'But they never understood that you wanted peace occasionally?'

Now she was surprised by his subtlety. 'How did you know that?'

'Don't forget, I've seen quite a lot of children who've had to move into another family. Quite often there are strains that no one suspects, even, or especially, in what appear to be well-balanced families. You'd be surprised at the number of times I've had to recommend counselling.'

'I don't need counselling!' The sharp words slipped out before she could stop them.

'I'm sure you don't,' he said easily. 'Tell me about your father.'

'I never met him. Apparently he died when I was seven. Sal once described him as a smooth, evil so-and-so and said the world was a better place with him dead.'

John smiled. 'Sal sounds a forthright woman. I'd like to meet her.'

Laura decided to ignore the hint and went on, 'Sal offered to train me as a hairdresser, but I'd always wanted to be a children's nurse so I trained as an SRCN and here I am. A perfectly normal, boring story.'

'Yes, it is,' he said slowly. 'Why do I think that there's more to it?'

'You're just imagining things,' she said. She picked up her glass again. It was time for her to drink up and get out.

'Do you think all men are like your father?' he asked. 'Is that why you go out with them so seldom? A gorgeous girl like you must get plenty of invitations.'

Stung, she said, 'I do go out with men when I want to!' Then she added honestly, 'But not very often. I'm perfectly fulfilled with my life as a children's nurse.'

'It's a good satisfying career. But there is more to life.'

Once again, something she didn't mean to say slipped

out. 'And I don't like tough, big, masculine men. And don't flatter me—I'm not gorgeous.'

'Oh, yes, you are,' he said softly.

Finally Laura managed to finish her drink. 'I enjoyed that,' she said rather quickly, 'but now I have things to do. May I get you another drink before I go?'

'Only if you'll have one with me. If not, I'll walk you across to the nurses' home.'

'There's no need,' she gabbled. 'I've enjoyed our chat but—'

A half-desperate voice behind them said, 'John, I've been looking everywhere for you.' They turned to see a harassed-looking man in the door of the Dragon Bar. Laura recognised him as Mick Lally, a conscientious but not very confident house doctor.

Mick waved a cardboard folder at John. 'You said you'd look through my paper and— Oh, hello, Sister.'

It was her opportunity. 'I'm just going, Mick, but you and John can stay for a chat. Bye!' Before John could argue she was making for the door.

Just before she went through it she turned to smile. On John's open face there was an expression that rather worried her. She'd forgotten how perceptive he was. He knew he'd upset her, and he wanted to know why. She'd have trouble with John.

'See you soon,' he said, and raised his hand.

She felt slightly as if she'd let him down as she hurried across the lawns towards her room. The story she had told him was perfectly true. It just wasn't everything. As she unlocked her door she wondered if she should tell him the whole story. He was kind and he'd be sympathetic. Then she blinked. Not for four years had she thought of telling anyone else. What was he doing to her?

* * *

Next morning she was the efficient Sister McLeod again. For a change she wasn't working one of the usual early, late or night shifts but an ordinary day, starting at nine and finishing—well, who knew when? Today John was holding the paediatric diabetic clinic—when children with diabetes came in for a check-up and a friendly word of encouragement.

David Miller had insisted that the clinic was user-friendly. The rooms were painted in bright colours, there were magazines for the mothers and toys or games for the children. Music played quietly in the background.

Laura liked the work. She helped John with the examinations as he checked eyes and feet as well as the more obvious urine and blood sugar. She also took blood from a vein, rather than the more usual finger prick, to give a HbAlc test. This test showed the average blood glucose level over the past three months, indicating how well the patient was controlling insulin and diet.

One little girl was about to start injecting herself. So far her mother had given them, but under gentle prompting from the medical staff she was now prepared to let her daughter take over. As the mother hovered anxiously in the background John carefully took little Amy through the various stages—where to inject, how to pinch the skin, how far in to insert the needle. It took time—but it was time well spent and John, as well as Laura, smiled as the needle was withdrawn and Amy said, 'Easy-peasy.'

It was good to see people they had treated in the past now living happy useful lives. In a sense they were old friends and Laura was pleased to see them.

One child, Barry Brent, didn't turn up. 'It's unusual for people just not to come,' she said to John. 'If they can't manage it they usually let us know.'

She leafed through Barry's case notes. 'He used to come with his mother, but apparently she's been sent to Kalex Hall and he now lives with his father.'

'I see,' said John, and he and Laura looked dubiously at each other. Kalex Hall was a hospital-cum-rest-home on the moors that catered for those who were severely mentally ill. There would be no point in trying to contact her.

'There's a phone number here,' she went on. 'I'll give it a try.'

She remembered Barry. He was nine, a thin frightened wisp of a lad, with a mother who looked just the same. His new address was in one of the vast blocks of flats on the other side of town. She remembered the place's nickname—Crack City.

'Who's that?' a surly voice answered when she phoned.

Laura explained in her most formal voice that she was the sister in charge of the diabetic clinic, and that Barry had missed a most important appointment.

The voice was uninterested. 'The hospital. Oh, there's no need to come in, he's OK. Perhaps in another three months.'

'We really would like to see him,' she said as persuasively as she could. 'Just to make sure everything's all right.'

'I tell you he's fine. Dr Spencer is looking after him. Now get off this line and stop bothering me.' The man rang off.

Laura squeezed her eyes shut and very gently put down the phone. There was no point in getting angry. Every nurse at some time came across ill-mannered, abusive or just plain evil people, but there weren't too many in paediatrics.

'Dr Spencer is looking after him.' That was another cause for disquiet. As a matter of course, many of the children who came into Robin Ward were referred to local GPs. Laura had come to know most of them, some in person, some by reputation. As a rule, doctors tended to stick together and could seldom be provoked into criticising a colleague. Dr Spencer was the exception. Nobody had a good word for him.

Still, she had to try. She rang Dr Spencer's surgery and spoke to the receptionist, explaining who she was and why she was calling. Five minutes later the receptionist phoned back and coldly informed her that she'd spoken to Dr Spencer; he had the child's interests at heart and there was no need to interfere.

Laura sighed. That was that.

'I think the child is in danger, John,' she said. 'He should be here for a check-up. We must be able to do something.'

John laughed. 'This clinic is really only an extra precaution,' he said. 'Don't forget, we hand over the care to the GPs. It's their job now, not ours. And we can't take over the policing of their work.'

'I suppose not,' she said, unconvinced.

Putting an arm round her shoulder, he urged her gently to the window. 'Look,' he said, pointing, 'that's the radiation block. We treat all kinds of cancer with some success now—even lung cancer—though the treatment can be unpleasant. And look who are outside the radiation block. People smoking.'

She was aware that he'd not moved his arm from her shoulders, and she found that comforting. He pulled her towards him so their faces were close. She could feel the warmth of his body, the long muscles of his thigh and chest and arm. 'There's only so much that we can do,' he said gently. 'Don't take too much on yourself. OK?'

'I suppose so,' she said. She wanted to stay in the shelter of his arms, but the door clicked behind them and he moved away as the clinic clerk entered.

The clinic finished early. John had an appointment with other senior medical staff and left promptly, without any personal message apart from saying to her, 'Enjoyed our drink last night, Laura.'

She felt dissatisfied. There were any number of things she could do, but she was going to do none of them. Instead, she went to her room and changed into jeans and duffle coat, then went out and caught a bus across town to the area known as Crack City.

It was a dreary, seedy area. She saw sharp-faced children, men who avoided eye-contact and no end of young girls, pushing prams. Feeling more depressed every minute, she wandered around, not knowing what she was doing or why she was there.

Then she had a stroke of luck. Outside a graffiti-daubed school wall she saw Barry Brent. She hurried over to him.

'Hello, Barry, remember me? I'm from the hospital.'

'Hello, miss,' he said, his eyes anywhere but on her.

'We expected you in the hospital this morning. Did you forget?

'I'm all right. My mam can't bring me any more and my dad says you only mess me about.' This wasn't the boy she used to know. Certainly he'd been shy, but she'd thought they got on reasonably well together.

'You're very quiet today,' she said, and this time, involuntarily, he looked up. She took in a deep hissing breath. There was a great bruise across the side of Barry's face from eye to chin—just the size of a hand, in fact. Trying to keep her voice pleasant, she asked, 'How did you hurt your face, Barry?'

Barry stared at the floor again. 'Fell over, miss.' There was a pause, and with the tiniest touch of hope in an infinity of misery he asked, 'You haven't come to get me back into hospital, have you, miss?'

Her heart wrenched. 'No, Barry, I haven't.' There was nothing else she could say. She watched him walk away.

Next morning Laura was on early shift again. She set about her duties feverishly, trying to hide the memory of Barry Brent walking away from her. He'd been happy in this ward. Halfway through the morning a soft voice behind her said, 'If you tidy up that linen cupboard any more it's likely to sue you for harassment.'

Her heart jerked as she turned to see John behind her, smiling at her obvious embarrassment. 'There's something worrying you,' he went on. 'You're not your calm, efficient self. Come and make me a coffee and tell me about it.'

'How do you know there's something worrying me?' she asked as they moved back to the ward office.

'I watch you a lot.' he said, 'because I like doing it. And I know something's wrong. Now, what is it?' She made him a coffee and told him.

'There's no holding you, is there?' he asked with wry admiration after she'd poured out her story. 'I think it's great, I really do, but you should only interfere so much.' He stopped and thought. 'Look, will you promise to do nothing more and I'll see what I can do to help this young Barry?'

'I'll promise,' she said, 'but what are you going to do?'

'Just leave it to me,' he said irritatingly. 'Possibly nothing.'

She saw little of John over the next two days. It often happened that way—the pressure of their jobs would keep them apart. Then she came in for change-over and there were notes of a new arrival. Barry Brent.

'Who admitted Barry?' she asked, skimming through the papers in front of her.

'There was a bit of a palaver,' the staff nurse said. 'There's been some trouble at home. Kid seems to have managed his diet himself, but there may have been some brutality. We're to keep him under observation a while, but I suspect he's happier now than he has been in weeks.'

She'd known Barry would be a perfect patient. Unlike some of the other children, who couldn't sit still for a minute, Barry did exactly as he was told, was invariably polite and so distant that he might have been on another planet. For a while Laura stood behind a screen and watched him, noting the cold, distant look she'd seen before. It was often a sign of abuse.

'I know what you're thinking,' a voice said behind her, and she turned to see John.

'Only because you're thinking exactly the same thing,' she said, and John nodded gravely.

'This isn't just chance,' she said. 'You've got him in here. I want to know what you did.'

He looked abashed. 'Well, it wasn't strictly a medical technique,' he said. 'I'm not sure what the BMA would think of it.'

'Come on, tell me!'

'Oh, well, I called in a favour. I know a fellow here who's quite high in the police force. I was at school with him. I phoned him up, told him a child's life might be in danger and asked if he knew anything about this man at this address. It turns out that he did.

'He organised a raid and caught Barry's father, pushing drugs. He's been remanded in custody. He's likely to go to prison and Social Services say there's no way he'll get Barry back. Apparently he's been using Barry to carry drugs for him. We'll get the lad better—then Social Services can find him a home.'

'For such a quiet man you can be quite ruthless, can't you?' she asked. 'I like it.'

Laura knew that sooner or later John would invite her out again. There was something in his manner—he treated her differently from the rest of their team. It wasn't much—a little extra consideration when they met, a hand resting just a little too long on her shoulder, a different kind of smile from the ones he gave the others.

And she liked it. She enjoyed their moments together and looked forward to seeing him, but she was still wary. She didn't know if she could commit herself fully to a relationship—and she felt that with John a relationship would have to be whole-hearted or nothing.

In spite of his large size, his sometimes tough way of acting, he was at heart a gentle man. She'd had plenty of invitations, some of them quite pressing, from similarly built men. She'd turned them all down. The few dates she'd had in the past four years had been with older or physically less imposing men. They'd been safe.

Perhaps she shouldn't go out with John. It wouldn't be fair to either of them.

When the invitation did come it was an unusual one. She was sitting at her desk when he walked in, and she had to admit there was a slight thrill, a definite lightening of her spirits, when she saw him for the first time in three or four hours.

He put down two green tickets in front of her. 'I

checked the roster. You're off on Friday night. The Russian State Orchestra is playing a Tchaikovsky night in the civic hall. I know you like Tchaikovsky so let's go together.'

She was rather flustered. This wasn't the kind of invitation she'd expected. 'How did you know I like Tchaikovsky?' she asked.

'The first time I ever spoke to you on the phone there was *Swan Lake* playing in the background.'

'You remembered that?' she asked, surprised.

'I remember a lot about you, Laura,' he said softly, and she had to look away.

With a finger she moved the two tickets backwards and forwards. She noticed that they were good seats. Listening to the orchestra from there would be magnificent, but... 'John, it's very good of you to ask me and I would like to hear the programme but you should know I just don't go out with men. Well, not very often.'

'I'm not asking you to ''go out'' with me,' he said cheerfully. 'I'm inviting you as a fellow music-lover to share my enjoyment of a concert. You know it's always more fun when you're with someone.'

She was tempted. 'You've already bought the tickets—and they're expensive.'

'I was hoping you'd come. If not, I shall ask Nurse Billings.'

Both of them laughed. Nurse Billings had just started on the ward. She was willing, but thought and talked of nothing but pop music. She got on very well with the older children. Laura had found her with one of the patients' Walkmans clamped to her ears, fingers snapping, head bobbing, oblivious to the world. She'd had to tell her off, of course. 'On a ward, Nurse, ears are as important as eyes.' But she'd be a good nurse in time.

John felt Laura was weakening and pressed his advantage. Like a mock conspirator he leaned forward and murmured, 'If you come I'll buy you a box of chocolates. And you may rustle the sweet papers during all the quiet bits.'

There were things she should tell him, warnings to give, but instead she said, 'All right. I'd love to go.'

'Then I'm leaving before you change your mind.'

She wondered if it was a good idea, but the orchestra was certainly getting good reviews.

He was to call for her on Friday evening. She opened her wardrobe and looked inside dubiously.

She hadn't bought many clothes recently, usually being content to dress in jeans and sweater. Why should she buy clothes? She didn't go anywhere much.

There was a dark blue silk dress, high-necked and long-sleeved, that she'd bought for a sister's wedding last year. She'd worn it with a hat Sal had insisted on lending her. She tried on the dress, then hurried down the corridor to her friend, Sister Joan Peet.

'Yes, it does look a bit stark,' Joan said, critically surveying an uneasy Laura. 'Not quite the thing for a night out on the town.'

'I'm not going for a night out on the town,' Laura mumbled.

'Take that off and try this on. No, I'm not showing you till you can see yourself in the mirror. You'll look stunning.'

From behind, Joan threw a dress over Laura's head and pulled it down. There was the long whirr of a zip being fastened up the back.

'Now you really are somebody,' Joan said.

'I can't wear this!'

It was a cheongsam, a Chinese dress in purple and gold brocade. There were no sleeves and it was slit to the thigh. Laura knew Joan was right—she did look stunning in it. Just for a moment she felt pain. She'd have liked to be the kind of girl who could and would wear a dress like this. But she wasn't. She reached back for the zip.

'This is just not me and I'm not wearing it. Have you got a scarf or something that I could tie round this blue dress?'

Joan knew she was beaten. 'There's a crimson one somewhere. Now, it's good to see you stepping out. Where are you going and who are you going with?'

She had known there would be a friendly interrogation. 'I'm going to the Russian concert. With...with John Hawke.'

'Dr Hawke! John! You've landed him! Every nurse in this place will hate you. He's turned down all sorts of offers from others, you know. Says he just wants to be friendly.'

'I haven't landed him and I do just want to be friendly. We both like music and we're going to a concert. We're just—'

'Don't say just good friends. If you do I might hit you.'

'Well, we are,' Laura mumbled.

She was beginning to wish she hadn't come. The nurses' home was a friendly place, but a hotbed of gossip. Everyone would know where she'd been and with whom. Clutching the crimson scarf, she escaped back to her own room.

John had said he'd pick her up at seven. She sat in her room with her coat on from six onwards, keeping watch out of the window. When she saw his car appear she hurried down the stairs to meet him on the steps outside.

'I would have called for you,' he said mournfully. 'There was no need to wait outside.'

'It's nice to be punctual. Besides, I live on the top floor. You might have been subjected to harassment on the way up.'

'I might have enjoyed it. You don't harass me very much.'

'Come on,' she said, patting his cheek. 'We'll be late.'

There was an undoubted sense of occasion at the civic hall. There were several couples in evening dress, and she felt pleased she had made an effort to dress up. John was wearing a dark suit and pristine white shirt. It was the first time she'd seen him in formal clothing and she thought he looked good, the complete up-and-coming consultant. Fortunately he still had the same blithe smile, and was flaunting a floral tie of epic brilliance.

'I like your tie,' she said. 'It's…different.'

'Different! Is that the best you can manage? Laura, this tie makes a statement. Shoes, suit and shirt—all are dreaded doctors' clothing. But the tie…' He bent to whisper to her. 'The tie shows I am different. I'm a medical twentieth-century equivalent of Lord Byron. Mad, bad and dangerous to know.'

She giggled. 'It's a lot to cram into one small piece of cloth.'

There was a change in his mood when she took off her coat. She realised he'd never seen her in anything but her uniform and the casual clothes she wore in the park.

Perhaps the blue silk dress hadn't been such a bad choice after all. It clung to her figure, suggesting and accentuating her curves. The colour went well with her dark eyes and hair. With an odd thrill she realised that other men were looking at her, while pretending to look for friends or partners.

'You look ravishing,' John murmured, 'you really do.' There was a throb of sincerity in his voice that she found both exciting and disturbing.

'Let's find our seats,' she said. An undercurrent of feeling was rolling between them. Too much was being felt but not said.

They sat, and with a smile he gave her the promised chocolates. Like so many of her nurse friends, she loved chocolate—loved the taste as well as the burst of instant energy that it gave. They had an enjoyable nut cluster each as the orchestra tuned up. Then the music started and the chocolates rested untouched on her lap.

The Russian State Orchestra played from the soul. She was shaken, moved as she felt the blackness of despair, the clarion call of hope, the sunburst of growing love. She was unaware of tears, shining in her eyes. When she snatched a glance at John she realised he was as rapt as she was. When he took her hand and squeezed it she squeezed back. It was something else they could share.

She'd heard all the music before, but never played with such passion. At the end there was applause that seemed to go on for ever. The orchestra responded by playing three encores. Then it was time to go and they drifted out with the crowd, an elation too deep for words filling them.

He put his arm round her. 'Would you like to go somewhere for supper? Or a drink perhaps?'

She shook her head. 'Not really, but I will if you want to. I'm still dancing round Swan Lake.'

'I know the feeling,' he said soberly. 'Shall we just drive around a bit?'

'I'd like that.' She'd said it. She was committed.

He drove her out of town and up onto the moors. Vaguely she noticed his driving style. It was like the man himself. He didn't jerk, was always polite to other road users and yet they seemed to move along in a remarkably efficient manner.

In time they reached a high point, and John turned off the road onto a layby where they could park and see the town spread out below them. They sat for a while, looking at the cross-hatching of gold and silver lights. They traced the town's main roads and looked for the darkness of Seddon Park and the concentration of stars behind it that indicated the whereabouts of the hospital.

It was cosy in the car. Laura felt warm, relaxed and happy to be with the man by her side.

'That was a lovely concert,' she said after a while. 'Thank you so much for taking me.'

'Taking you made it so much more enjoyable.'

Cautiously Laura said, 'Yes, going with someone is always more fun.'

'I didn't go with just someone. I went with you.'

He'd put his arm behind her head, and now he started to stroke her hair, his hand curving round the side of her face so his fingertips gently touched her cheek.

At first she held herself rigid, but then the gentle caress calmed her and her head lolled back against the seat. Her eyes closed, and her other senses were instantly keener. She could hear the distant hum of traffic and, nearer, the sigh of the moorland wind, eddying round the car. There was the faint smell of leather in the car and, more exciting, *his* male smell, half expensive cologne, half body warmth.

But most of her attention was focussed on his touch.

She hadn't thought that the delicate contact of skin on skin could produce such unendurable pleasure.

It was almost a relief when his hand dropped back to her shoulders and he turned towards her. Somehow she managed to slip both arms around his waist inside his jacket. She could feel the heat of his body, his heart hammering as he pressed against her.

No one else could have kissed her as John did. He was gentle, tentative at first, his lips soft and warm. Whatever inhibitions she might have had soon broke away, and she revelled in his nearness—in the pleasure he could give her, in the power she had over him.

His hand strayed across her arm and shoulder, with the most feather-light of touches cupping her breast. She almost cried out in ecstasy. It felt as if dress and bra weren't there, as if the warmth of his hand held her naked body. In her excitement she felt her breast burgeoning under his palm, the tautness exquisitely exciting.

Laura could tell John felt the same mounting passion. He pulled her willing body to his so she could feel the heave of his chest as he panted her name, feel his arousal, the thud of his heart.

There was nowhere she wanted to be but here, no one she wanted to be with but this man. She was transported to a plane of being she'd never entered before. And all this, she thought feverishly, from one kiss. What if they—?

The thought seared across her consciousness like a hot iron laid on soft white flesh. She dared go no further. It wouldn't be fair. The feeling of floating on a cloud of sensuousness evaporated. She was sitting in the front seat of a car, slightly cramped. Her body stiffened.

She said nothing to John—it wasn't necessary. A man

as sensitive as he knew something was wrong at once. Somewhere deep inside she felt sorrow for him and guilt for her own behaviour. She'd led him on.

He leaned back in his own seat, keeping hold only of her hand. 'Laura, Laura,' he murmured hoarsely, 'there's no need to worry. I was too sudden with you. I'm sorry if I caused you pain.'

There was such regret in his voice that she felt the tears ease out of her eyes. She could guess what it had cost him to stop, and here he was blaming himself for what was her fault.

'No, John, it's not your fault, it's mine,' she mumbled. 'I shouldn't have come here. I shouldn't have come out with you at all. I'm just not…good…with men.'

'Ah,' he said, and there was an infinity of sadness in his voice. She knew he didn't understand, and there was no way she could explain. She half wished he'd get angry with her. It would make her misery easier to bear. But she knew he wouldn't.

'I do like you,' she said, 'and I want to be your friend. I'm sorry about tonight. Will you take me home, please?'

'I'll do whatever you want me to.' The car eased backwards onto the main road.

There was nothing she could think of to say as the car curved down into town again, and yet the silence was unendurable. He must have felt the same. His free hand rubbed her arm and he said, 'Come on, cheer up, Sister McLeod. We've had a good time and you do like me really, don't you?'

'Yes,' she said quietly. 'I like you more than anyone I've met for years. It's just that—'

He held up his hand. 'We'll stop there. I've made

progress. Don't let anything else worry you. In time all will be well.'

'I hope so,' she said, knowing it wouldn't be.

The rest of the journey home was easier.

Her apprehension returned as they neared the nurses' home. Would he expect an invitation in for coffee? Would he…? She needn't have bothered. 'You could drop me off at the—' she started hesitantly.

'Don't even suggest it,' he said.

At the nurses' home he opened her door and walked her to the little entrance hall. Once inside he said, 'Laura, I've really enjoyed tonight. We've had a good time together and I want to go out with you again soon.'

'But—' she protested.

'No buts. Goodnight, Laura.' He took her hand, squeezed it and was gone. She looked after him in bewilderment.

It was Friday night, and most of the nurses who weren't working were out on the town. Somehow Laura managed to get to her room, without being grabbed and interrogated. For once she fell into bed, without having a shower. She slept instantly.

CHAPTER FOUR

LAURA woke early. For a moment she lay in bed, a small smile on her face. She wasn't sure why but she was contented. Something nice must have happened to her.

Even when she remembered the events of the night before she didn't feel too despondent. John was an understanding man—he'd forgive her. They could work something out.

There was a rattle on her window. She opened her eyes fully to see that it was raining. The sky was full of dark clouds, grey and threatening. Her happiness evaporated. She wasn't looking forward to today.

Her swim did little to cheer her up, and then there was the walk to the station and the suburban line across town to Gilmour, the prosperous area where she'd been brought up. Most people thought Gilmour a pleasant place to live. Laura now hated it—Gilmour meant Gilmour Rugby Club.

She walked into the big kitchen of the house where she'd spent so much of her youth.

'The prodigal returns!' Sal shouted, and grabbed her in a big hug. 'Larry, we don't see enough of you. You're looking well.'

'It's good to see you too, Sal,' Laura said, hugging her aunt affectionately. Feelings of guilt welled up in her. No one could have been better to her than Sal had.

'Here's a pinny, start work.' There were bowls of salad and plates of cheese, ham and beef on the kitchen table. As usual Sal was making sandwiches for the club to sell. The club had definite ideas about a woman's place. The ladies' committee was, in effect, a catering committee.

Laura put on her pinny and started to butter rolls. How many weekend mornings had she done just this with Sal? They seemed endless.

'Not engaged yet, no man on the horizon?' Sal queried, working efficiently. 'I think we're about ready for another family wedding.'

Laura smiled. 'I'm not engaged yet, but I did go out with a doctor last night. We went to that Russian concert.'

'You did? What's his name? Is he nice? When can I meet him?'

Laura smiled at Sal's barrage of questions. 'We're just friends who like music. There's nothing else in it.'

'Pity. But it's a start to hear of you going out with anybody.' Sal eyed Laura's rather severe French plait. 'I could do your hair. That style doesn't do much for you.'

'It's handy on the ward. Doesn't get in my way.'

'Hmm. Remember when I sent you to school with that bubble cut?'

'I remember. Miss Prentice told me off, said it was most unsuitable for a schoolgirl. Then she came to see you and wanted a bubble cut herself.'

'She still comes to me,' Sal said cheerfully. 'Always asks after you. Are you sure you don't want me to do something with that? You've got lovely hair—you should make more of it.'

'You can do it when and if I get married, but there's no chance yet. Where's Robert?'

'He's at the club—where else? He won't drink till after the match, though. He's just gone to catch up with the gossip. Got to keep in touch.'

Catch up with the club gossip. Got to keep in touch. Laura shook her head.

It had just stopped raining when they walked down to the grounds. As before, Laura didn't want to go into the clubroom. It brought back memories. Sal looked at her oddly, but said nothing. Laura pulled up the hood on her anorak, thrust her hands deep in the pockets and paced up and down the touchline. She wanted to see Robert, but otherwise she wished she were somewhere else.

Sal rejoined her as the players ran onto the pitch. Laura waved at Robert, taller and leaner than his two heavyweight older brothers. The game started and Laura stared at the sky.

After a while the rain started again, heavier than before. The players were soon covered in a thick layer of mud and it was hard to tell them apart. After a couple of minutes Sal said, 'I don't care if he is my youngest son, I'm not staying out in this. Coming for a drink, Larry?' Laura shook her head.

The game progressed—she supposed. She took what shelter she could at the foot of the stands with two other spectators and gazed dumbly at the mud-covered figures, running, slipping and heaving at each other. Dimly she became aware that the two men sheltering with her were home supporters, who'd recognised Robert.

'Young Buster Wilmot is a really dirty player,' one of them said with pleasure. 'He's got that ref fooled. Look, he's at it again.'

Laura knew the speaker was a well-known local solicitor. She didn't like what he was saying or the note of delight in his voice. It's only a game, she felt like pointing out. Why bother cheating?

She could just make out Robert's long, lean form. She

could see what he was doing, dashing around the side of a scrum.

The whistle blew and the game was stopped once again. Patiently she stared at some pigeons who were sheltering in the stand behind her. Then she felt a ripple of unease run through the crowd. It was hard to say why, but suddenly there was a quietening, an alteration in the muttered comments around her.

Beside her the solicitor said, 'I didn't like that. I know he was asking for it, but I didn't like the way he went down.'

Laura looked. The players were gathered in a group in the centre of the field, looking down at someone. The trainer was already there. Then there was a gasp from the crowd and she saw a well-dressed man hurry onto the pitch, a coat over his shoulders and a bag in his hand.

'That's not good,' said the solicitor. 'They've sent for the doctor.'

Anxiously she scanned the players. There was no sign anywhere of Robert's lanky frame. 'Who's hurt?' she asked the solicitor, apprehension growing inside her.

'I'm afraid it's Buster Wilmot,' the man said. Then he caught a glimpse of her anguished face and reassured her. 'He'll be all right now. The doctor's gone to him. No, don't go…'

She ignored him and ran onto the wet field, slipping and nearly falling as she neared the group of players. She pushed through the muddy men, now docile and apprehensive.

Robert was lying on his back on the ground, pain and panic in his eyes. The doctor was kneeling by his side, a neck brace on the top of his bag. It was a ridiculous thing to think but for a moment Laura worried that his neat trousers would get stained. As she watched, the doctor replaced his mobile phone and said, 'The ambulance is on its way. Will someone go to the gate and guide it here?'

Laura stared at the stooping figure disbelievingly. The doctor was John Hawke. What was he doing here?

Another player, a member of the opposite team, was squatting behind Robert's head, cradling it carefully so he couldn't move it. Robert's eyes fixed on her, and when he spoke his voice was high-pitched, showing his panic. 'Larry, my neck hurts but I can't feel anything else. There's nothing there. I can't feel anything.' Terror gripped Laura. She knew what that could mean. An injury to the spinal cord. Paraplegia, even quadriplegia. Robert could be paralysed for life—or even die. However, she was a nurse so she forced herself to sound confident. This was the younger brother she'd grown up with—he needed her love and support.

'You've had a bit of a shock, Robert,' she said, hoping there was no tremor in her voice. 'Just lie there and take things easy. We'll have you in hospital in no time.' She knelt by his side and took his hand. 'Now, try not to move.'

John's eyes flicked upwards. 'Laura,' he said with obvious amazement. Then he went on quickly. 'I need a nurse. Support the head while I slip on this brace.'

The muddy figure holding Robert's head was only too pleased to let Laura take his place. She tried to forget this was her half-brother and concentrated on being a nurse, anticipating John's movements. He eased the brace round Robert's neck, then tightened it precisely.

'What are you doing here, Laura?' he asked.

'Robert—this man—is my brother.'

His dark eyes looked into hers compassionately. 'I see,' he said. He didn't offer any words of encouragement. Both of them knew how serious the break could be. There was nothing Laura could say. She couldn't cope with the shocks, hammering into her one after the other.

'We could move him into the pavilion,' the trainer said doubtfully.

'I suggest not. Perhaps he'd be better not moved until the ambulance arrives.' John's voice was authoritative and the trainer nodded his assent.

Someone came rushing from the pavilion with blankets and a silver foil insulator. Laura helped wrap them round Robert's chilling body. She took his hand again and squeezed it, telling him for the tenth time not to worry and that everything would be all right. There was no answering pressure. She knew it was a lie. Last night John had squeezed her hand. Now things were terribly different.

In the distance she heard the sound of the ambulance siren, getting nearer. The vehicle was directed to the side of the pitch, and soon there were two paramedics, hurrying over with a special stretcher.

Under the paramedics' direction Robert was carefully lifted onto the stretcher and his head taped to it to keep it motionless. Laura said she would go to hospital with him and asked if someone would tell his mother who was in the bar.

'I'd better come too,' John said.

The ambulance journey was a nightmare. Laura could tell that the driver was taking particular care, trying to reconcile the need for haste with the need not to shake Robert and thus make his condition worse.

She crouched by the stretcher, holding Robert's hand. 'I can't feel anything,' he kept murmuring. 'I can't feel anything.'

'Don't worry, I'm sure everything will be all right. You're just badly bruised, that's all.' She said it with as much conviction as she could muster but she knew she was trying to reassure herself as much as Robert. The nerves controlling the body passed through the spinal column. Any damage could result in permanent paralysis.

His face was white under the mud. She pulled a handkerchief from her pocket, licked it to moisten it and tried to wipe the caked earth from around his mouth and eyes. She remembered her mother doing just that. Robert shut his eyes, but tears forced their way through.

They drove through the gates of her own hospital. She felt sick as they did so. Her role here had now changed. Before, she had been one of the carers, a professional doing what she could for those who were ill and for the inevitable anxious relations and friends. Now, she was another of those anxious ones and she didn't like the feeling of powerlessness it gave her.

A doctor and nurse were waiting outside Casualty— the ambulance driver had radioed ahead. They took Robert straight to the resuscitation room. It took only a moment to confirm John's diagnosis. Robert was then swept straight through the department for X-rays of the skull and cervical spine. Laura remained behind for a moment to book in his details.

John had disappeared but now he reappeared, a vexed expression on his face. 'Young Mick Lally wants me on the ward,' he said. 'I strongly suspect it will be nothing but—'

'You've got to go,' she said. 'It's been…it's been marvellous, having you near me.' She reached forward and hugged him quickly. 'But I can cope now.'

'You always cope. I'll see you when I can.' And he was gone.

I always cope, she thought sadly. If only he knew.

After a few minutes the casualty doctor came to see her. She'd seen him before and he knew that she was a hospital sister. It made conversation easier. 'It's beyond us,' he said abruptly. 'I've sent for Charles Whitrow—fortunately he's on call this weekend. He'll be here in half an hour. D'you want to sit with your brother?'

'Yes, please.' She knew that everything possible was being done. Charles Whitrow was the consultant in charge of the regional neurosurgical unit at the hospital—a man with an international reputation. If anything could be done for Robert he could do it. If anything could be done.

She sat in the little curtained cubicle. Someone had cut off Robert's rugby kit and sponged his face. It was now pale and he looked awfully young. He lay there with his eyes closed and Laura sat by him, praying silently that all would be well. A nurse brought her a plastic cup of coffee, squeezed her shoulder in companionship and slipped out.

Waiting was the hardest part. She had always known it.

The curtains were swept aside abruptly and there was Charles Whitrow, a nurse and two other doctors behind him. He smiled briefly at her and then looked down at Robert. 'Could I see the X-rays, please, Nurse?' Then he turned back to Laura. 'Sister McLeod, isn't it? From Paediatrics?'

'Yes,' murmured Laura, pleased that he knew who she was. 'And this is Robert Wilmot.'

'Ah. Boyfriend?'

'No. He's my brother.'

'I see. Well, we're going to move Robert straight to
Theatre and when I've operated we'll move him to Ward
27. There'll be no news for at least two hours so why
don't I see you in the waiting room there? Now, you're
a nurse. You know this could be very serious indeed?'

'Yes, I know,' she said. 'How…how bad is it?'

After a moment's thought he pointed to the X-ray.
'There's an unstable fracture/dislocation here at C6,' he
said. 'The spinal column has moved. It's going to need
internal fixation—pinning, in fact.'

'So he'll be—'

'Let's wait till after the operation, shall we? But spinal
shock…'

She got back to Casualty Reception in time to meet
Sal. With her was Clive, her oldest son. Clive was now
an accountant, a big man who still occasionally played
rugby. But now, in spite of his expensive tweed overcoat
and carefully groomed hair, he looked diminished.
Laura's heart went out to Sal. She'd never seen her look
so lost. For once the super-confident Sal didn't know
what to do.

Laura took charge. 'He's being seen by the consultant
now. There's nothing we can do for a while so you'd
better come across to my room for a while. It's more
comfortable than the waiting room.'

'Is he going to be all right?' It was every mother's
cry.

Laura knew it would be ultimately cruel to raise false
hopes. 'He's been hurt pretty badly, but he's got one of
the best men in the country looking at him.'

'I see.' Sal breathed forlornly. She had understood
Laura's unspoken message.

Laura took her two relations to her own room, and
made them tea. 'You'll have sugar for once,' she said

firmly. 'You're both slightly shocked. I don't want you fainting on me.' Then she phoned the sister of Ward 27 and explained the circumstances. The sister promised to ring back just before Mr Whitrow would be available. It struck Laura that for the first time in her life her relations were looking to her for a lead. This was her territory— she knew what to do. In the middle of her misery she felt a tiny spark of pride.

They waited much longer than two hours, but then the orthopaedic sister phoned and Laura shepherded her two charges over to Ward 27. They were shown into a tiny waiting room and ten minutes later Charles Whitrow entered, still clad in his theatre greens. He shook hands as Laura made the introductions. She shivered as she observed his cautious manner. It wasn't the approach of a man with good news.

'I'm afraid Robert has suffered a very severe insult to the spinal cord,' he said, and showed them the X-rays. 'You will notice the displacement of the vertebrae here. I've done what I can.'

'So have you cured him?' Sal burst out. 'Is he going to be all right?'

He shook his head. 'I've stopped things getting worse. His respiratory system, for example, should be quite functional. But there's a limit to what we can do. There is always some chance, of course, but it would be wrong of me to raise false hopes in you. I'm afraid you must come to terms with things. I'm sorry, but he's likely to be paralysed.'

'Paralysed,' Sal gasped. 'How long for?'

Laura knew what the answer would be, but it still came as a shock. 'There is always some hope, but in this case, I'm afraid, very little. Robert will probably be paralysed for the rest of his life,' he replied softly.

The sister took them to look at Robert's unconscious
form. He was being specialled, meaning someone would
look in on him every few minutes, take his temperature
in case infection developed and check and record the
other readings. To Laura the bank of monitors, the ITU
line, the arterial line, measuring blood pressure, the
check for blood gases, the urine monitored by catheter,
were all commonplace, part of her life. But to Sal and
Clive they were something seen only on television,
frightening in their implications. 'He won't die, will he?'
Sal whispered.

'No,' Laura said firmly. 'Things aren't as bad as they
look. A lot of people are monitored like this after an
operation. Now, there's nothing we can do here. We
might as well go home.'

Clive drove them back in his Jaguar. Laura sat in the
back with Sal, holding her hand. After twenty minutes'
uneasy silence Sal said softly, 'Robert can't live in a
wheelchair, Laura. He'll go mad. You know what he's
like.'

Laura did know, and she realised Sal had a mother's
understanding of her child. 'He'll have to take things
one day at a time,' she urged. 'Don't start worrying yet
about what might happen in the future.'

Sal wasn't to be consoled. 'I just know he won't
cope.'

Back at the house the usually bustling Sal slumped in
the corner of her kitchen. Clive fetched her a brandy.
She sipped from the glass then left it on the corner of
the sink. It was left to Laura to make tea, deal with
callers and fend off enquiries. Clive went to fetch his
wife. They would both stay with Sal for a few days.

Clive drove her back to the hospital. She had found a
replacement for her evening shift and had offered to stay

with Sal, but everyone said they'd rather she went back to work. She knew what they were feeling. Laura was their contact in hospital—she knew people and how things worked. 'We're going to rely on you a lot, Larry,' Clive said as he dropped her off at the nurses's home. 'You can cope with this a lot better than any of us can.'

With a slight shock she realised that it was true. She was no longer the little sister, to be looked after and— without any intent—patronised a bit. For the first time in her life she could offer something back.

She went upstairs, changed out of her still mud-stained trousers and glanced at her watch. It was only half past eight, but the past few hours had seemed an eternity. She knew she couldn't rest so she went back to Ward 27.

Robert was lying there, still unconscious, still connected to the monitors by his bedside. She looked at the readings. Everything was as normal as could be expected. There was nothing she could do or see, but she sat there anyway.

Eventually she decided to go back to her room. She asked the sister to phone her if there was any change, then walked through the double swing doors. Sitting on a bench outside was John Hawke.

He was dressed casually in black trousers and sweater. His face was pale. As she approached him he opened his arms and it seemed right to lean against his chest and let him wrap his arms around her. He was warm and comfortable—she wanted to rest there for ever. But she didn't. Reluctantly she eased herself away, and tried to smooth her straying hair.

'What were you doing at the match, John?' she asked. Even to herself her voice sounded high, unnaturally polite.

His answer was calm. 'They always have a doctor handy for matches. I was asked if I'd do the job. I used to play, you know.'

At one time the knowledge that John was a former rugby player would have been enough to put her off him for good. But now things were changing.

'Thank you for what you did for Robert,' she went on in the same voice. 'He's had his operation now and we…we…'

'I know about the operation. I've had a word with Charles Whitrow. Have you been home with your stepmother?'

'She's not my stepmother, she's Sal,' Laura said, knowing she wasn't making sense. 'Yes, I've been home and they want me here to sort of keep an eye on… I mean…'

'How long since you last ate?'

That was a stupid question—no, it wasn't. She'd had plenty of cups of tea or coffee, but nothing to eat. She wasn't hungry.

John knew there was an answer in her silence. 'You're trying to carry your family, aren't you?' he asked shrewdly. 'Take on their worries as well as your own. They're turning to you as you're the medical expert. And it might be good to be recognised—but you're finding it an awful strain.'

She was too tired to do anything but nod.

'Come on, you can lean on me for a bit. Just go with the flow.'

Unresisting, Laura let him lead her downstairs and sit her in his car. It only took two minutes to drive to his flat. She had a vague impression of a plant-lined foyer and a small lift, then she was sitting on a soft leather couch with a glass clutched in both hands. John had one, too.

'The Macallan,' he said, 'one of the great whiskies. If you don't like the taste then think of it as medicine.'

She drank it fast and the taste never registered, but it was certainly medicinal. She was dragged out of her stupor and forced to recognise what had happened. Robert, her brother, had broken his back. He would be paralysed for the rest of his life. She laid her head on John's shoulder, held him to her and wept as she hadn't wept since she was a child.

John didn't move as the tears shook her. He didn't say anything either but gently stroked her back. When finally the sobs turned to sniffs he offered her a large white handkerchief. 'Blow,' he commanded.

She didn't, but wiped her eyes. 'Could I use your bathroom, please?'

When she saw her reflection she winced. She looked a red-eyed mess. After she'd washed her face and splashed cold water on it she felt better. She did what she could with her hair and dabbed on a touch of make-up. She felt more herself.

When she re-entered the living room there was the entrancing smell of warm bread. On the coffee-table was an open bottle of wine and two plates with bread, salad and fresh salmon.

'John, I—' she started but he shook his head.

'Don't say anything. After you've eaten we can talk…if you want. But eat first. You'll feel better.'

She hadn't realised how ravenous she was. And he was right. After the meal she felt better. She looked at him quizzically. 'You're treating me as a patient, aren't you? You knew I was bottling things up and you gave me that drink on purpose. You wanted me to cry.'

'I didn't want you to cry but it did you no harm. You were in some kind of shock. Sometimes it's not good to keep feelings to yourself, to repress them.'

She thought for a moment then nodded. 'I've nursed children who never showed any emotion. Often they're the abused ones. They're emotional bombs, just waiting to explode.'

She realised how much better she felt. She had been hungry as well and John had recognised that. She owed him so much that she felt she could tell him about…

At first the very idea frightened her. It was her secret, and she had kept it to herself for four years. But as she thought about it, it became more and more possible. She knew it had affected her. Perhaps it would help if she told someone. And John was the one she wanted to tell.

'John, you know when we went out on the moors, and you kissed me, and I said I wasn't…wasn't good with men?'

'I remember.' His voice was soft, calming.

'Well, there's a reason. You might think it's silly, but it's made me a bit wary of men. Something happened to me once.'

He didn't move, but she knew he was instantly alert. She had all his attention. His voice was still soothing as he asked, 'Do you want to talk about it?'

'I think so. I've never told anyone before and it might help. It happened at a rugby club dance, the May Ball, in fact…'

It had been a wonderful, early summer evening, the air warm after a perfect day. The party had spread all over the club. There had been dancing, drinking in two or three bars, even a mad game on the pitch played with a balloon instead of a ball.

She had bought a new outfit for the occasion—a white silk dress which, she knew, suited her. In it she felt confident and attractive. She'd never worn it again.

Laura had danced several times with Eric Myers, a vast young man who'd played for the first fifteen. The club had been very proud of him as he'd played several times for England. Laura had found him amiable but a bit of a bore.

She hadn't realised that all the other girls there had thought him a catch. She'd gone to the Ladies, largely to escape from Eric for a while.

'How're you getting on with our Eric?' Val Knowles asked, trying unsuccessfully to conceal the envy in her voice.

Laura shrugged. 'He's OK, I suppose. I don't really like drunks—they're boring.' She knew she sounded a bit prissy, but she didn't know just how much she'd irritated the other girls.

Outside Eric handed her a glass of fruit punch taken from the giant bowl. It was quite nice, fizzy and tasty and quite harmless. Laura didn't know Eric had poured a double vodka into it.

After that things got mercifully vague. She knew she drank more than she'd intended. Nobody noticed her situation. Everyone else was drunk and eventually she must have passed out.

She woke in what was wittily called the retiring room. Usually it was for storing kit. Now there were half a dozen half-comatose girls around her, lying on benches or piles of netting. She heard the thump of drums in the background. When she squinted at her watch she realised that it was only half past two and the ball was still going on.

She turned to Val who was sitting near her, looking

distinctly the worse for wear. 'What happened?' she asked.

Val shrugged. 'Apparently you had a great time. Eric Myers carried you in half an hour ago, saying you were marvellous.'

'I don't remember a thing,' said Laura, bewildered.

'You shouldn't mix happy pills with drink,' suggested Val. 'But you'll be all right now.'

'I didn't take any pills!' Laura croaked.

'Oh, yes, you did. I could tell the signs. Half the people here have tried one. Don't let it worry you, Laura.'

Desperately Laura tried to remember. Eric must have spiked her drink. She knew nothing would make her take so-called recreational drugs. 'I think I'll go home,' she muttered.

'Good to see you letting your hair down, sweetheart,' Val called after her.

Somehow she staggered to her roomy house nearby and let herself in. The rest of the family were still enjoying themselves. Only then, in the privacy of her own bedroom, did the full horror of what must have happened struck her. And she could remember nothing.

She started to get undressed. Her white dress buttoned up the front, but the buttons were fastened in the wrong order. Her bra was loose—somehow it had come undone. Her tights were torn and a great ladder ran from waistband to inside her knee. Her plain white briefs were inside out. Eric must have undressed her and... And what? She couldn't remember. Perhaps she'd been entirely willing. Whatever had happened had occurred while she'd been unconscious. She had no one to ask, no one to confide in.

She bathed, scrubbing herself in a frenzy, and then sat up all night with the light off. She heard the rest of the family come in. When one of them popped his head round the door to see if she was all right she lay down and pretended to be asleep.

'I came into hospital the next day and saw a lady doctor. She wasn't very sympathetic, but she said I was still...still a virgin. It was my fault for drinking too much. And since that day I've been, well, wary of men. I just can't help it. And I don't like to go to the rugby club any more, which means I don't go to see Sal and my family.'

She was glad he didn't tell her that she was being silly or say that it was all in the past. Instead, he asked, 'Do you feel better for telling me?'

She thought about it. 'Yes, I do,' she said. 'It's made it all a bit more manageable.'

'I'm glad that you felt you could tell me.' He looked at her speculatively. 'This isn't the time to go into it any more. You look drained, Laura. This must have been one of the most traumatic days of your life.'

'It has. And you've been good to me.'

'D'you think you should take tomorrow off?'

Now that was a foolish idea. 'Certainly not! I may be upset but I'm capable of work.'

'No one doubts that and perhaps work would be the best place for you.' He paused. 'It's getting late, Laura, so would you like to stay here for the night? I've got a spare bedroom.'

They looked at each other. She knew it was an innocent suggestion but suddenly the atmosphere between them changed. She wanted to stay but she knew it would be better if she went. 'I think I'd better go back to the nurses' home,' she said breathlessly. 'You don't mind?'

'Perhaps it would be a good idea. Come on, I'll run you back now.' Outside the home he kissed her, a kiss that started as a sign of friendship and quickly turned into something else. This time it was he that pushed her away gently. 'We have things to talk about, Laura,' he said hoarsely, 'but not tonight. Goodnight, my love.'

'Goodnight, John.' She walked into the nurses' home. It had been a long, long day.

CHAPTER FIVE

LAURA was on earlies next morning. Surprisingly, she had no difficulty in waking. She lay in bed for five minutes, thinking about the previous day. Obviously Robert came first to her mind, but then she thought of John and the story she had told him. Perhaps her life would change now for the better. She felt guilty at the elation she felt.

She forced herself to have her usual swim, and then rang Ward 27 just before she walked across to work. The night sister said there had been no change in Robert's condition and he'd spent a reasonably comfortable night. She had used similarly reassuring phrases herself when relatives had called in about ill children. For the first time she realised just how meaningless they were.

She rang Sal with the news and arranged to meet her that afternoon for a visit. Sal still sounded stunned. 'I'm glad you'll be with me, Larry,' she said. 'I don't want anyone else there.'

'I'll do whatever you want me to,' Laura said. Once again she felt a half-guilty thrill—it was good to be needed.

She was a nurse now, and her own problems had to take second place to the care of her charges. There was the drugs round, and dressings to supervise. She pushed Robert to the back of her mind.

Mid-morning John tapped on her door and peered round it. When he saw that she was alone he entered, shutting the door behind him. There was no one looking so it seemed quite in order to let him kiss her.

There was an expression on his face that she'd seen before—hesitant, as if absorbed by some difficult puzzle. 'Good morning, Laura,' he said softly. 'I hope today will be an improvement on yesterday.'

'I'm sure it will,' she gabbled. 'John, you were good to me yesterday. I feel I landed you all with my problems.'

He shook his head. 'I did nothing I didn't want to.'

'Well, I'm grateful. You know that for the next day or two all I'll be able to do is think about Robert?'

'That's understandable, but when you can think of your own life I want to be involved. I very much want to be involved.'

She wanted to kiss him again and knew by his half-smile that he'd guessed her thoughts. 'There will be time for us,' he said.

She looked at him more closely and saw lines of fatigue down the sides of his face and at the corners of his eyes.

'Did you get much sleep last night?' Laura asked.

'Not a lot. I lay there, thinking of what had happened to you and what you'd told me. I was trying to imagine the effect it had had on you.'

'I think I need to have a normal life for a while. Not think of anything, but concentrate on nursing. It's what I'm good at.'

He looked disappointed and she thought for a moment he was going to disagree, but eventually he nodded. 'It's probably the best thing for you for a while. Now, Sister, I'd like to have a quick look at Alan Carton. I think we might be sending him home tomorrow.'

'Thank goodness for that,' she muttered. Alan was a

sweet little boy but he bounced around like a rubber ball. If there was mischief to be got into, Alan would be in it.

They stepped into the corridor and walked to Alan Carton's bed. 'Look, Sister, I've got the photos of me at the summer camp. They've just sent them to me. That's me up a mountain and I'm in a canoe as well!'

It was a welcome relief—a small, excited child in space pyjamas, thrusting pictures under her nose. Alan was eleven years old, a diabetic in for his usual half-yearly check.

She and John examined the proffered photographs. She thought it was typical of John that he would take time to talk to his charges with such interest. To him they were people not cases.

'I recognise this mountain, Alan,' he was saying. 'It's by Grasmere, isn't it? Helm Crag?'

'The Lion and the Lamb,' Alan corrected him. 'That's the lion and that's the lamb and that's me.'

'Very impressive. Is that your jacket?'

'No, they lent them to us from the camp. Looks good, doesn't it?'

Laura had to smile at the photograph. The background was the rock John had recognised. In the foreground there was Alan's face, grinning hugely. The rest of his head and body was concealed by a voluminous orange garment, stretching down to mid-calf.

'I'm hoping to go again next year. But I suppose others will have to have their turn.'

'We'll have to see what we can do,' she said carefully. 'It depends on a lot of things.'

'I suppose so— What?'

From down the corridor there came a cry. The fa-

vourite mid-morning television programme was on and
Alan was missing it.

'You look at them and give them back to me,' Alan
said hurriedly, and shot off to the TV room.

In fact, both Laura and John were interested in the
pictures. They showed young people taking part in a
variety of outdoor pursuits—walking, canoeing, sailing,
singing round a campfire. A close observer would have
noticed that there seemed to be rather a lot of helpers
with them.

'It's my favourite doctor and nurse! Good to see you
both.'

Laura and John turned. There was Harry Roscoe, a
great smile on his face, his hand outstretched.

'Morning, Mr Roscoe,' John said, shaking the offered
hand. 'Timmy's doing all right now, I hear?'

'I've just been to see him and, yes, he is doing all
right. Thanks to you two.'

'It was Laura here, not me—' John started, but Harry
interrupted.

'I know exactly what happened, and I'm grateful.
You've both done me some good, too. I've altered my
life. I now spend more time at home with the family.
Timmy now has a father as well as a mother. Made a
big discovery, in fact. There are people other than me
who can be trusted to run my business. I work half as
hard as I used to—and I still make as much money.' He
laughed, a great bellow that had John and Laura smiling
too.

'You'll probably enjoy life more this way,' John said.
'Work to live, don't live to work.'

'Yes. And you do a thirty-five hour week, too,' Harry
pointed out drily. 'What are the photographs?'

Laura passed them to him. 'Young Alan there went

on a special holiday camp for diabetics last summer,' she said. 'It's good for them to mix with others with the same problems—makes them feel less isolated. And some of them wouldn't get a summer holiday otherwise. Timmy might be interested in a year or two.'

Harry looked through the pictures. 'Sounds like a good idea,' he said casually. 'Who pays for it?'

She shrugged. 'Whoever can. A lot of staff give their time free—we need quite a high ratio of helpers to children. I've been a couple of times. There's some kind of a grant from various charities. We manage somehow.'

'Nothing from the NHS?' Harry asked.

Laura and John laughed. 'No,' they said simultaneously.

'How many children do you take away?'

'Well, not as many as want to come. There's—'

'Sister, I'm a bit worried about Laurel May. She seems very hot and she won't sit up or talk or anything. I wondered...'

It was Natalie Platt, the Project 2000 nurse, her expression anxious. 'I'll come at once,' Laura said. 'Will you have a look, John?'

'You're busy. I'll leave you,' Harry said. 'I'll be in touch.' He turned, and John and Laura followed Natalie down the ward.

With Laura and Natalie looking on, John examined the little girl. Then he decided to take no action. It was typical of him, Laura thought, that he took Natalie out of earshot and carefully explained why he thought it best. He was a good teacher.

In the afternoon Clive brought Sal to the hospital, and Laura took them to Ward 27 again. Robert was conscious but had been given a mild tranquilliser. The doctors didn't want to depress his respiration. His eyes opened slowly when they walked into his room, but there was little intelligence in them and they soon closed again.

Sal was as fearful as ever. Her eyes took in the bank of equipment, the tubes and leads monitoring his body. 'He must be dying,' she whispered, 'for him to need all this.'

Laura shook her head. 'This is all straightforward stuff. They're just keeping him still and quiet, and these machines mean he doesn't need a nurse with him at all times. In a few days he'll be in an ordinary bed and talking like he always did.'

Laura reached out and took his hand. His eyes opened again, but this time there was the spark of recognition in them—and also fear.

'Talk to him,' she whispered to his mother and brother. 'Even if he doesn't take it all in, it will help him.'

But Sal couldn't speak. She sat, her body racked by silent sobbing. Laura put a comforting arm round her.

It was Clive who spoke, in a hoarse voice very different from his normal confident tones. 'You'll soon be up, Buster, playing again. The lads decided last night that they'd put on a charity match for you. You get the gate money and we'll have raffles and so on. You've got a lot of friends there…'

Perhaps it helped. Robert showed little sign of hearing them, but they had tried to talk to him. After a while Laura suggested that they left. Apart from anything else, she didn't like the effect the visit was having on Sal.

'Quite a few friends at the club were asking about him,' Clive said as they walked back towards his car. 'When can they come and see him?'

After a moment's thought Laura said, 'He'll be aware of things in a day or two. There may be some…problems when he realises fully how badly he's been injured. He'll need family support then, but I don't think that seeing his well friends will be a good idea.'

There was a short silence, and then Clive said heavily, 'That seems very possible. We'll do whatever you say, Larry.'

'Laura, have you got a proper sister's uniform? Not those pyjama-type things you wear on the ward?' It was John on the phone. She sat in her office and considered this rather odd question.

She hadn't seen him for two days. She was spending most of her spare time with Sal when she visited Robert. It was good to hear his voice.

'Yes I have a sister's uniform,' she said. 'Why do you ask?'

'All will be revealed—just trust me. You're free this afternoon, aren't you?'

'Yes, I'm still on earlies. I'll finish in an hour. But—'

'You can do me a favour. Get in a taxi and come to 47 Lamb's Lane. It's in Burlowe. And bring your uniform with you. Can you get here by three?'

'John Hawke, you're irritating me! Why d'you want me and my uniform?'

'Because you look gorgeous in it. And a little mystery should creep into every life, Laura. See you at three. I'll be waiting to pay for your taxi.' He rang off, leaving her very intrigued.

Burlowe was a Victorian area of the town, full of large stone mansions. Most of them had now been turned into upmarket businesses. Laura knew of several consultants who had private surgeries out here.

The taxi turned into a driveway and drove through a very carefully groomed garden. There was plenty of money here. A discreet board stated they were at Lamb's Lane Studios. Studios?

As promised, the minute the taxi stopped someone came out to pay, but it wasn't John. A figure in a black pencil skirt and starched white blouse smiled at her. A badge on the blouse stated that she was Millicent Ward, Receptionist. 'Miss McLeod? Dr Hawke is sorry he's not here to meet you but he's shooting at the moment. Won't you come inside and watch for a moment?'

John, shooting? She was more perplexed than ever.

Her little suitcase was carried for her and she was led through several rooms until they came to a padded door with a red light overhead. Millicent Ward put a finger to her generously coloured lips and gently eased the door open. Laura was taken to a chair and told to watch and please not make any noise.

The room was mostly in shadow. The far end was brilliantly lit by arc lights and Laura could see cameras and a microphone hanging overhead from a boom. Men were sitting, watching, behind the cameras. And John was centre stage against a light blue background.

He was holding what she recognised as a plastic model of the pancreas. As she listened he explained its construction, its functions and what could go wrong with it. She heard him say, 'And here are found the islets of Langerhans...'

Of course, she'd heard similar lectures before when she was studying, but she'd never heard a lecture as clear as this. John was a natural teacher. He spoke clearly, but didn't talk down to his audience or oversimplify. He explained how diabetes was caused, and what could be done. Finally he said, 'But that's enough theory. Let's go and look at a real live patient.' Then, just like Laura had seen in so many films, someone shouted, 'Cut.'

The arc lights went out and the lights in the rest of the room came up. John saw her and walked over to her, smiling. She couldn't help it—her heart beat faster. She hadn't seen him for two days, and that was two days too long.

'You didn't know I was a film star, did you?' he asked. 'This is my director, Marcus Fox.'

Marcus was a tall, thin, bald man, clad in the most shapeless jacket she had ever seen. He shook hands with her, then stared intently at her face. 'Yes, I think so,' he said to John. 'I think so, indeed. Have you brought your uniform, my dear? How about in half an hour?'

By now Laura was totally confused and a touch annoyed. John noticed this and said, 'I'll take Laura for a coffee, Marcus. See you in about half an hour.'

She was taken upstairs to a lounge and John fetched her a coffee. 'Film people drink more coffee than even hospital staff,' he said, 'but they spend more money on it.' She tasted hers and found he was right.

'Now, you're wondering what is going on, and why I'm here and why you're here?'

'Something like that. I feel as if I've been kidnapped.'

'I wanted to get you here without preconceptions. Now, a firm called Gladstone Films is trying to make a series of medical instructional films. Training films, if you like. They're specially designed for use in parts of Africa and South America where staff don't easily get to training hospitals—or, indeed, any hospitals at all. If necessary, they'll be dubbed into other languages.'

He paused and she saw the enthusiasm in his eyes. It was a quality she loved in him.

He went on, 'I wrote the scripts for a couple of them

while I was in London, and tried a bit of presenting. It's interesting work. Anyway, the plan was put on hold for a while, but now Gladstone Films is trying to put out a pilot. And I'm involved again. Marcus has hired this studio for a week.'

'And what about me and my uniform?' she asked suspiciously.

'Ah. Sister McLeod, if you were given the chance of helping a nurse who was faced with a diabetic child for the first time in her life, you'd help that nurse.'

'John, you're trying to manipulate me!'

'Of course I am. And I don't feel too bad about it. Now, read this and give me your professional opinion on it.'

She took the paper he offered her. It was a script, and started, 'After diabetes has been diagnosed, nursing the child is all-important…' There was a brief account of the nursing problems of diabetes and the script ended, 'And now we'll look at a child in the ward.'

'It's very good,' she said honestly. 'Like the talk you gave before, it's clear and helpful.'

'Good. It lasts about three minutes. I want you to change into your uniform and read it into the camera.'

'But, John, I can't—'

'How d'you know if you've never tried? I'll take you to where you can change and then you can look in at Make-up.'

Laura changed into her uniform. She knew she looked well in it, the severe lines suiting her face and figure. In Make-up an efficient lady wrapped a cloth around her and patted powder onto her face, changed her lipstick, tidied her hair. Then she was taken downstairs again and placed in front of the light blue background.

'I don't know how,' John said, 'but they'll insert a

background later. Now, just imagine you're talking to the nurses on your ward.'

Mysteriously, behind the camera, the words she had been reading appeared on a big screen. John retired and Marcus took over.

'Laura, I know exactly what you're feeling. First of all, it doesn't matter if you get things wrong. Everybody does, and we can try again. Second, remember you've got something that's worth sharing. Two hours ago children's lives were in your hands. As John said, pretend that you're talking to a young nurse new to the job. Ready?'

Of course she was nervous. When she started to speak she faltered on the first two sentences, but Marcus waved her to carry on and she didn't think the rest was too bad. The second time she spoke she nearly got it right. Just one hesitation at the end. The third time Marcus said she was perfect.

A few minutes late she was seated with John, Marcus and some others, looking at a vast television screen. And there she was in her uniform, talking to a non-existent junior nurse. At first it was a shock—she'd never seen herself on screen before—but then she decided she hadn't done too badly. The words were clear and the message got across. 'We'll turn you into a film star,' John said.

Marcus said, apparently sincerely, that she'd done well and he hoped they might work together in the future. John said he was finished at the moment and asked if he could take her to dinner. She shook her head sadly. Suddenly her life took on a darker shade. She had duties, responsibilities.

'I'm meeting Sal later,' she said. 'I can't let her go to see Robert without me.'

'Then we'll go to the pub and have a sandwich.' She thought she'd like that.

Sitting in the Seddon Arms, with a vast plate of bread and cheese in front of her, she looked appraisingly at John opposite her. The afternoon had passed in a whirl— she'd hardly had time to think. But now there were questions he had to answer.

'This afternoon was something completely new,' she said. 'I found it fascinating. And I didn't think once about my problems. You knew that would happen, didn't you? You deliberately set things up so I would be taken out of myself.'

'Yes,' he said bluntly. 'Actually, you were a very good speaker—I thought you would be. But I organised it primarily to give you a respite. You work too hard and you worry too much. Your eyes look tired.'

'I'm worried about my brother,' she flared, 'and about the rest of my family.'

He leaned over to stroke the back of her hand. 'Sometimes I just want to…do things for you.'

'I'm my own person, John, and there are decisions that only I should take.' She decided that she was being too hard on him. 'But I really enjoyed myself. Tell me more about these films. How did you come to get involved in them?'

For a moment she thought he looked ill at ease, but his answer was clear enough. 'Somebody I met in London. You know how it is with film-making. For every film made there are a dozen good ideas that get half started and then there's not enough money or something. This was one such idea that got lost and now they're trying to get it off the ground again. I think it's a very worthwhile project.'

'I thought your introduction was really good,' she told him. 'You're a natural on screen.'

John smiled sheepishly. 'If you're a children's doctor you have to be a bit of an entertainer. It goes with the job. Now, didn't I ought to drive you to meet Sal?' It was time to go.

He dropped Laura outside Ward 27 and she had to wait for Sal as she was ten minutes early. It had been a fascinating afternoon and she thought she'd enjoyed herself more than she would have thought possible.

John was a fascinating man. She kept discovering sides to him that she'd never suspected. The apparently open man was really quite complex. With a slight shock she realised he had manipulated her.

Certainly it had been in her own interests and because he cared for her, but she still wondered if it was good for her.

Over the next three days they met briefly—professionally—on the ward. John was always with someone, and only occasional guarded eye-contact suggested to Laura what he was thinking. She wondered why at least he didn't phone her. On Saturday he did. She was still at work, still on earlies.

His voice seemed abrupt, harassed even. 'Laura, could you get round to my flat this afternoon? There's something we have to discuss.'

'Not a career in show business, is it?' she said cheerfully. 'Not making me a film star too?'

'Nothing like that, nothing at all, but it is important. Could you get here for four o'clock?'

'Well, I could but I'd like to know why—'

'Trust me Laura. I'll see you then.' He rang off, leaving her half angry, half intrigued. Was he manipulating her again?

He greeted her gravely. She noticed he was dressed semi-formally, in dark trousers, white shirt and college tie. 'I'm so glad you came, Laura,' he said. 'This means a lot to me.'

He took her coat, seated her in his living room and poured her a coffee. 'Sometimes it's hard, being a doctor,' he said. 'You have to make decisions and you're never entirely sure what the consequences will be. Sometimes your decisions mean pain, and that's hard to take. Especially if you're proved wrong.'

She didn't like that at all. 'You're worrying me,' she said honestly. 'Can we start now?'

There was a moment of silence, then he said, 'Laura, I want you to meet an old acquaintance.' He knocked on the kitchen door.

Someone entered. He was fatter, older, sleeker. Some of his hair had gone. But she could never forget who it was. It was Eric Myers. The man who had drugged her, undressed her, done she knew not what to her while she was unconscious. John had invited him here.

Laura couldn't speak. She wouldn't look at Eric, and when she glanced at John he seemed cold and remote. She wondered if she'd ever know the real John Hawke. Did he know what he was doing to her?

Eric fidgeted, obviously uncomfortable. Laura wondered what she could do. She couldn't speak. All she could do was sit, horrified at John's betrayal.

John said, 'This is a case conference. There are facts we have to uncover and everything will be confidential. I will start by retelling Laura's perception of what happened four years ago.'

Suddenly she could speak. 'Perception!' she spat. 'I

know what happened four years ago. John, whatever I told you was in confidence. You're breaking that confidence. You're not fit to be a doctor.'

He'd been pale already, and she thought he grew even paler. 'There will be time for recriminations when we've finished, Laura, but for now just listen!'

She hadn't thought him capable of snarling at her in that way. He took a breath and then said, 'Four years ago…'

He told the story—the strong punch, the pill, her awakening in the back room. The clinical way he described the events made them seem even more sordid than she would have thought possible. For a while she wondered if she was going to be physically sick. 'Drink some coffee, Laura,' John rapped, and, numbed, she did so.

'That's what you remember,' John continued. 'Now I want Eric to give his version of the same events.'

'I don't want to hear his version of the same events,' she cried. 'I told you, I can remember.'

'Just listen, Laura. Eric?'

Even she could appreciate how uncomfortable Eric Myers was. He wiped the sheen of sweat from his forehead and loosened his tie. His voice was a mumble. 'First of all, I'm sorry. I'm ashamed of my actions, and now I'm more ashamed when I see what effect they've had, but I'm not quite as bad as you might think.'

He leaned forward and drank from the coffee John had poured him. 'I really fancied you, Laura, and, yes, I did spike your punch with extra vodka. But I didn't put a pill in your drink. Some other idiot had them at the party and was dropping them into strangers' drinks. His idea of a fun time, we found out later. Laura, you passed out—that was all. I did nothing to you. In fact...in fact, I was being sick. Then I carried you into the back room to sleep it off.'

She was angrier than ever, and even more embarrassed. 'I happen to know that's not true,' she said. There was no way she could bring herself to mention her disturbed underwear.

John could. 'The reason she doesn't believe you, Eric,' he said, 'is that her underwear was interfered with. Someone had undressed her.'

If possible, Eric looked more wretched than ever. 'I'm sorry, Laura,' he said again, 'but it wasn't me. It was the girls at the party—you know, Val Knowles and the others. They'd never seen you drunk before, and they wanted to give you a bit of a shock. I think they thought you a bit of a snob—and I know Val fancied me. Anyway, they undressed you and dressed you again. I think they meant to tell you after a couple of days, but you were never seen at the club again.'

Was that it? Laura thought. Had she worried over a stupid prank by some stupid girls?

Eric stood. 'I think I'd better go now,' he said. 'Laura, you've no reason to think well of me, and I apologise again for being a drunken lout, but I assure you I'm telling the truth.' He hesitated. 'I'd like you to know I'll say nothing about this meeting. God knows, I'm not very proud of myself. Goodbye, Laura, Dr Hawke.'

She sat motionless as John showed him to the door, unable to control her reeling thoughts. When John returned she simply asked, 'Do you believe what he said?'

'Absolutely,' he said. 'Don't you?'

She nodded. John studied her and said, 'Just sit quietly a minute.' He flicked a switch and the soft sounds of Mozart filled the room. 'It's a lot to think about. Your life's just changed, Laura. I hope it's for the better.'

She closed her eyes and let the music wash over her. Her heart was beating far too quickly and she tried to control her rapid breathing. There was so much to think about.

After ten minutes she opened her eyes. Her body had reacted and now she felt limp, powerless. 'Could I have another drink of that whisky, please?' she asked.

The drink trickled down her throat, warming her and making her think instead of merely feeling. 'You've got some explaining to do,' she said.

'I have. First of all, I broke your confidence and I didn't like doing it.'

'You manipulated me.'

'Possibly. But I did it in your interests.'

'Tell me how you came to meet…Eric Myers.' It still came as an effort to say the name.

'It wasn't hard to do. I went to the rugby club and had a casual word with some of the members. From your description I worked out that the man had to be Eric Myers. And the story itself—it had seemed a bit wrong to me. I went to see Myers and we talked quite calmly. I was glad we did. We'll never be friends, but he isn't a wicked man. The three girls who undressed you are all now living reasonable lives with no idea of the harm they've done. I haven't spoken to them—I saw no need.'

'I can't take it all in,' she said.

'There's plenty of time. Just let things come to you gradually.' He put his arm round her shoulders and she leaned against him.

'You're changing my life,' she said.

CHAPTER SIX

LAURA didn't go for a swim next morning. Instead, she lay in bed and thought. There had been too much happening to her recently, and she needed to get her ideas in order. Early morning was the best time.

Robert, of course, must still be her first concern, although she knew there was little she could do for him. For a while she could act as a buffer between him and the family and the reality of the situation, but ultimately they would all have to face up to the bleak prospect of him spending the rest of his life in a wheelchair. She winced.

What about yesterday's revelations? After she'd left John's flat she'd been in a daze, not fully able to comprehend what she'd learned. Her wariness of men had been totally unjustified. She felt an easing of her spirit, as if something tight had suddenly loosened. Suddenly she knew that never again would she instinctively recoil, as she had with John when they'd been in his car.

She stretched and smiled, a warm, self-satisfied smile. If he took her in his car again she knew she would... She grew pink at the thought.

What about John? He was the most attractive man she'd ever met, as well as being warm, good-tempered and a superb doctor. She felt good with him. Occasionally, though, she caught glimpses of a different John— of someone who was tough, willing to take risks, ready to back his own judgement. Never would she have thought that he would have gone looking for Eric Myers.

With something that might have been a qualm she realised that there was an awful lot about him that she didn't know. Still, it might be fun finding out.

Her new-found optimism was dampened a little when she got on the ward. Natalie was willing and hardworking but still needed more practical experience. Laura had given her the task of changing a dressing, after making sure that she'd observed the procedure three or four times already.

Natalie did well at first. For a while she talked to eight-year-old Malcolm, reassuring him and trying to get him to relax. Then she took off the old dressing from the great gash across Malcolm's abdomen and carefully cleaned the site. Laura nodded approvingly. The job was done thoroughly but with regard for the patient's feelings.

Now for the new dressing. Natalie washed her hands, put on fresh rubber gloves and opened the sterile dressing pack on the trolley by the bed. She picked up the dressing, fumbled and dropped it onto the bed. With a little frown at her own clumsiness she picked it up and made to put it on the wound.

'Nurse,' Laura asked wearily, 'what happens to a sterile dressing when it's dropped on an obviously unsterile bed?'

Realisation shook Natalie. 'Oh,' she said, horrified, 'it won't be sterile any more.'

'It won't. Now go and get another pack.'

She'll learn in time, Laura thought. All she needs is experience.

At mid morning there came a message from John who had been called down to Casualty. Could they admit a ten-year-old boy? He had collapsed in the school playground and taken some time to revive. The head teacher had sent for an ambulance and had gone herself to fetch the parents who weren't on the phone. 'I'll see to a bed at once,' Laura said.

As she replaced the phone she wondered if she'd imagined the extra hint of warmth in his voice. She thought not.

Twenty minutes later she and John were looking down curiously at the sleeping form of the boy. All they knew about him so far was his name—Brent Padgett—and the fact that he had collapsed in the school playground. A blood test in Casualty had suggested anaemia, but there had been no indication as to the cause. There now appeared to be no life-threatening condition, and before any detailed examination John wanted to speak to the parents, who were on their way.

'He's very brown,' Laura said, 'and, look, there's not a bit of fat on him. You can see every bone. It's almost as if he was suffering from starvation. He's even got the slightly distended stomach that comes with lack of food.'

'He has, indeed. Feel the soles of his feet,' John suggested.

She did so. The skin was hard and calloused. 'He doesn't wear shoes?' she asked.

'Very seldom, I would say. I came across cases like this when I worked for a time in Africa. There it would have been simple malnutrition, but here I'm not so sure. Young Jim in Casualty thought it might be malabsorption, coeliac disease even. That's why he sent for me.'

'We need to talk to his GP,' Laura said. 'He must know something about it.' She knew about malabsorption. Sometimes the intestines could not absorb iron or folic acid or vitamin B12. The result was very similar to malnutrition—weight loss, anaemia and fatigue.

'Where is our child? Why has he been brought here?'

It was an angry voice, but a cultured one. Laura turned to see a thin, bearded man, dressed in rough workman's clothes. Behind him was a woman in an ankle-length skirt and hair down to her waist.

'I am Brent Padgett's father and I demand to know where he is!'

Quietly John said, 'He's here, Mr Padgett. Why don't you have a look at him and then we can go to Sister's office and have a talk.'

'There is nothing to talk about. I am this child's father and I shall be removing him from this…place at once.'

'Mr Padgett, your child is—'

'Hospitals cause more diseases than they cure. I refuse to leave Brent in one. We are taking him now!'

Laura knew that John was angry, but his voice was calm as he said, 'Mr Padgett, this child is now in my care. We can discuss his case quietly or I can call the police and Social Services and say that I believe your son has been subjected to systematic abuse.'

'You medical fascist! You wouldn't dare!'

'Oh, I would dare, Mr Padgett.'

Laura thought it was time she did something. Moving round to the woman, who had so far remained silent, she said, 'We really are worried about Brent, you know. He's not in a good state.'

'Yes, but Carleton has his own ideas about bringing up children. We only sent him to school because we were forced to. Carleton says that the educational system and the medical system cram children into moulds. They should be more natural.'

There's nothing natural about starvation, Laura thought, but she merely said, 'If you could calm your husband down I am sure we could talk about things in a rational manner.'

'Yes, perhaps so.' The woman seemed to brood a minute, then moved forward. To Laura's amazement her voice cracked out like a gunshot. 'Carleton, stop this foolishness at once. We will listen to what the doctor has to say.'

'But, Miranda…'

'I bore him. I will take his decisions until he is old enough to take them himself. We will listen to the doctor!'

There was a moment's fraught silence, then the man said, 'Yes, dear.'

'If we may borrow your office, Sister,' John said, keeping a determinedly straight face.

It was half an hour before he came down the ward to speak to her. Pulling a face of mock agony, he said, 'They've gone. Mother wanted to stay with Brent but father said he felt stifled in this atmosphere. I think she decided he was entitled to a small victory so she went with him.'

'So, do you know what is wrong with Brent?'

He sighed. 'Treat the family not the child. I've got a good idea. They live on a smallholding that his father bought them. He's got ideas about being self-sufficient and about diet. He's an educated man and he told me that ultimately he wanted the family to live on nothing but brown rice and peas. Madness!'

She understood now. 'So it's not an illness. Brent's just not getting enough food.'

'Not enough of the right kind of food. They are vegans and have nothing to do with animal products whatsoever. They won't take supplements or pills either. It's a guess on my part, but I wouldn't be surprised if it was vitamin B12 deficiency. We'll do further blood tests—that will show.'

'How did you persuade them to leave Brent here?'

Laura had forgotten that in spite of his relaxed appearance John could be as hard as teak. 'Well, the mother was vaguely willing and I convinced them by telling them that if they removed the child he would probably die. And that I'd see that they were both prosecuted for manslaughter. Come on. I know what we're looking for now.'

The message came five days later while Laura was busy on the ward. Would it be convenient for Sister McLeod to come and see the hospital chief executive—perhaps some time this afternoon? Like all the CE's messages, it was courteous. Laura frowned at the slip of paper handed to her by Natalie. When humble sisters were summoned to see the head of the hospital it wasn't usually good news. She rang the CE's secretary.

'If you could make it for half past two,' the secretary said, 'then the others can be here.'

'The others? What others?' Laura asked, more mystified than ever. 'You know, I've no idea what this is about.'

'I'm sure Dr Black will explain,' the secretary said tactfully. 'I know he's looking forward to seeing you.'

So it's not bad news, Laura thought, and busied herself with ward affairs.

Perhaps unusually, most people in the hospital liked and trusted the chief executive. He was seen as a man trying to do a hard job properly. When cuts had to be made he made them reluctantly and only after a considerable fight.

At twenty past two Laura presented herself at the CE's office. She was still in uniform but had taken a couple of minutes to freshen up, tidy her hair and make sure there was no indication on her dress of the hard session from which she'd just come.

To her surprise John was sitting in the office, his legs sprawled out and his head back, looking as relaxed as he always did. He also looked surprised as Laura entered.

'I'll just make coffee and then you can have it all together,' the secretary said, and left the room.

She'd hardly seen him for five days. She knew he'd been working hard, covering for David who'd been on a conference. Now they looked at each other and something, some spark, flashed between them. They both knew that they had more talking to do, that their lives somehow were converging. But now wasn't the time.

'This is exciting, isn't it, Laura?' he asked, showing no sign at all of being excited. 'Do you think we've done something wrong and we're going to be told off?'

'It's just like being outside the headmistress's study, isn't it?' she said with a giggle. 'I keep on wanting to make sure my hat's on straight. But I don't think we've done anything wrong.'

'No,' he said gloomily. 'We haven't. A pity, really. Just think of the fun we could have had.'

'Behave yourself,' she scolded. 'Do you know who's in there already?' They could hear the hum of voices from behind the broad mahogany door.

He shook his head. 'No idea. I've only met Dr Black twice—when I was appointed. He seemed a pretty reasonable sort of chap to me.'

'He is. Very keen on getting outsiders involved in the hospital. He says we serve the community and the community should be encouraged to give a little back.'

'Seems a good idea, though I've met a few consultants who wouldn't be too pleased. Perhaps—'

'Ah, Sister McLeod and Dr Hawke. Please do come inside, both of you.' Dr Black—tall, white-haired, black-suited—had opened his door and was beckoning to them. He beamed as they passed him.

To their surprise David Miller, the paediatric consultant, was already in the room. He, too, smiled as they were given chairs. Then they all had to wait another few minutes as the secretary brought in coffee.

Finally the meeting started. 'Now,' Dr Black said, 'this is to be a pleasant meeting. All too often I meet staff only when there is some kind of crisis, but today there's nothing but good news and I must say I like it.'

Laura and John exchanged glances. It wasn't quite what they had expected.

'First of all, congratulations on what you did for young Timmy Roscoe some time ago. His father's spoken to me. He now has a high opinion of the medical staff here.'

'Laura deserves the praise, not me,' John said calmly. 'She spotted what was wrong.'

'No, I—' she started, but Dr Black stopped her.

'It doesn't matter now.' He grinned. 'Just don't put in for any overtime payments. What does matter is that Harry Roscoe is determined to do something for the hospital and he wants you two to help him. You know he runs Roscoe's Travel Shops? Well, he's offered to pay for ten diabetic children to go to America for a fortnight. If you two will go with them.'

'I've never been to America,' Laura muttered, knowing her comment was irrelevant.

She was astounded, and when she glanced across at John she saw that he was also having difficulty, taking in the news. 'Why us?' she asked. 'I mean, it's a very generous offer but aren't there other people who would do a better job?'

'Harry Roscoe thinks not. In fact, the offer is conditional on you two going with the children. If you two don't go neither do they.'

'I see,' said Laura, but she didn't.

'Let me go through the conditions. I've spent quite a lot of time with Harry recently—we're getting on well together. He's a very forthright man. It's easy to see the qualities that have made him a successful businessman.'

'Qualities that could be useful in helping to run a hospital such as this,' John put in slyly, and the chief executive had the grace to look slightly uncomfortable.

'He could be a loyal friend to us. Now, Harry has offered us plane tickets, travel, accommodation, entry to a variety of places like Disney's Magic Kingdom and the services of couriers while you're over there. I'd like to emphasise that you two will have nothing to so with the arrangements. Harry and I will see to all that.'

'It will cost him a fortune,' Laura gasped.

'Not really. You'll be going at an unfashionable time—the last week in November and the first in December. He has a lot of spare capacity then that he can't fill. And he'll be able to write off his losses as publicity. But still…ten kids will get a holiday. Now it's up to you two. I need an answer by tomorrow afternoon. The hospital will give you one week off—you'll have to take the other week out of your holiday entitlement. Do you want time to think about it?'

It was John who spoke first. 'I think it's a very generous offer. I'll happily go if my workload can be cleared.'

'I'll guarantee that,' David Miller put in.

'Sister McLeod? Do you want time to think about it?'

There were all sorts of reasons why she ought to think about it. Going abroad with John Hawke was one. But for ten sick children to have a holiday… 'It has to be John and myself?' she asked.

'It has. I did suggest that was perhaps unreasonable. Harry said it was his money and he'd spend it how he wanted.' Dr Black winced a little. 'I wish I could run the hospital like he runs his business.'

There was, of course, no doubt about what her answer would have to be. 'I'll go,' she said faintly. 'Please thank Mr Roscoe for us.'

'I'll certainly do that. Thank you, Sister McLeod, Dr Hawke.'

A dazed Laura and John were shown into the corridor.

'I think we need to sit and talk a bit,' John said. 'Shall we go to the Dragon Bar for half an hour? I'll ply you with extra-strong orange juice.'

'I think that might be a good idea.'

'Dr Black seemed almost more excited than we were,' he said, once they were sitting in a secluded corner, iced orange drinks in front of them.

'He's a driven man. He desperately wants the community involved in his hospital.'

'Harry Roscoe will be a useful ally. Why do you think he insisted on us two going with the children?'

She gave the obvious answer, even though she suspected it was not completely true. 'Because we helped Timmy?'

'There's more to it than that. He's deliberately pushing us together, making sure we have time with each other.'

'And with ten sick children,' she reminded him.

'And with ten sick children,' he acknowledged. 'But

we will be on holiday together, and in exciting surround-ings. Harry Roscoe doesn't look like Cupid, does he?'

She smiled. 'A travel agent, firing little golden arrows. No, he doesn't. Anyway, we're going abroad to work, not to...' Her voice trailed away.

'Not to fall in love?' He spoke softly, gently.

'I still don't know you very well. I think I understand you, and then you surprise me. I mean, it was a shock, and now I'm glad you dug up Eric Myers and things are fine. But I never dreamed you'd do anything like that.'

'I thought you were worth fighting for. Looking for Myers wasn't an easy decision.'

'Are you going to shock me again? Is there anything else about you I don't really know?'

Just for a moment she wondered if his eyes clouded, if a momentary doubt had struck him. Instantly, the im-pression was gone.

'You'll find out a lot about me while we're away. Do you know how many holiday romances blossom into full-blown love affairs?'

'John Hawke, I keep on telling you, we're going to work!'

He reached over to touch her wrist. 'A man can dream,' he said.

That evening she went as usual to visit Robert. She'd phoned Clive and told him not to bring Sal. The pair of them needed a day off. Sal was still having difficulty, coping.

By now Laura knew the names of many of the staff on Ward 27, and they knew that as she was a nurse herself they didn't have to maintain their usual profes-sional attitude. They could be honest rather than diplo-matic.

'How's he doing, Hilary?' she asked the staff nurse.

Hilary sighed. 'Not well, I'm afraid. You know how it is. When something like this happens you never can tell who's going to manage—or how well.'

Laura nodded. Different kinds of nursing had different problems. Quite often in orthopedics previously fit, healthy people had to deal with the prospect of a life of pain or paralysis. A surprising number of them coped. Some didn't—and made the nurses' and their families' lives a misery.

Robert was still in his side room, but was now sitting up. The drugs which had kept him semi-comatose had been withdrawn, and the consultant had decided not to give him any tranquillisers.

She smiled at him as she entered the room. 'What are you grinning at?' was his abrupt response. Carefully, she didn't let her smile slip. She had to be the strong one.

'I'm just pleased to see you,' she said. 'How're you feeling today?'

'How d'you think I'm feeling? On top of the world, of course.' There was raw bitterness in his voice.

She sat by the bed and took his hand. For a while they sat in silence.

He spoke first, and she shuddered when she heard him. His voice wasn't savage, as it had been before—she could deal with that. Instead, there was an acceptance, a resignation that seemed to be the result of much thought. His voice chilled her.

'I'm glad you've come on your own, Larry. You're the only person I can talk to. At least, you're the only person who'll be honest with me. You are honest with me, aren't you?'

'I try to be,' she said doubtfully. She knew too well

that when people asked for honesty they often didn't mean it.

He went on, 'Sal and Clive do their best but they just can't cope. The doctors and the nurses say that it's too early to tell yet, that I must wait and see. I'm not a fool, you know. All I want is someone to tell me straight that I'm going to spend the rest of my life in a wheelchair.'

'The doctors genuinely don't know,' she protested. 'You'll just have to wait and hope.'

'You know me, I've never waited for anything in my life.' Sadly, that was true. None of Sal's children was capable of waiting.

'You'll just have to wait for once.'

'I can't. Now, don't lie to me, Larry, you owe me that much. I calculate that out of a hundred chances there's just one that I'll ever walk again. Is that right?'

She struggled to find something to say, some way of avoiding the stark question he had posed her. 'It's not as simple as that,' she mumbled after a time. 'For a start lots of people in wheelchairs live happy—'

'I'm not lots of people. I'm Robert, your brother. It's not much I'm asking—a simple yes or no. Will I spend the rest of my life in a wheelchair?'

He wasn't shouting but there was a ferocity in his voice that shook her. She felt hunted. There was nowhere for her to go now. She knew she should refuse to answer, tell him that he'd have to wait, say that no one could foretell the future, but he held her transfixed, the force of his wide blue eyes pinning her to her seat. Weakly she said, 'There's a good chance that you'll have to spend quite some time in a wheelchair.'

'There. That wasn't too bad, was it? Don't you feel better for being honest?'

She didn't feel better at all. She felt that somehow

she'd failed in her duty both as a nurse and as a sister. 'You should pay more attention to the consultant than to me,' she quavered.

'I needed to get things sorted out in my own mind. I'm not going to spend the next forty years in a wheelchair. I'd rather be dead. You're the only one I can ask, Larry. I want you to get me something to take. Some pill or other to see me off.'

For a moment she didn't grasp what he was saying, then her mind reeled with the enormity of the idea. 'You...want...me to help you kill yourself?' she gasped.

His voice was now cold and passionless, as if he'd gone beyond emotion. 'That's exactly what I want, Larry. I know it's a lot to ask, but I certainly can't ask anyone else.'

'No, Robert! I can't and I won't! You've got your whole life ahead of you.'

'Call this a life? Life means walking, running, even playing rugby.'

'There's more to life than that! Listen, Robert, we've got a kid on the ward called Marion and she's paralysed and in a wheelchair. What's more, she's blind so she's learning to read Braille. And a nicer, happier little girl you couldn't wish to meet. I'll bring her over if you want so you can see her and stop feeling sorry for yourself!'

She wasn't used to this kind of situation. She didn't know whether she'd made Robert's mood better or worse. She was a nurse, not a psychiatrist, but she desperately wanted to do the right thing.

There was a long pause, she watched fearfully as he stared, stone-faced, at the opposite wall. Finally, a small smile touched his lips.

'At bottom you always were a tough little thing,' he said. 'I'd forgotten that.'

'So, no more talk about pills and things?'

'No more talk about pills. Well, not for a while, anyway.'

'Not ever! Now, d'you want me to read to you, like I did when you were a little boy?'

'*Just William* books! Have you brought any?'

'Only the paper, I'm afraid. But I could read the cartoons.'

Their mood was strained, but she thought the worst was over. She stayed for another half-hour until she saw his eyes closing, and knew it was time to leave. 'I'll be back tomorrow, Robert.' She leaned over to kiss him and then slipped out.

Outside she leaned against the wall, incapable of further movement. Hilary saw her and led her to a tiny waiting room. 'Just sit and cry,' she said softly. 'I'll bring you a coffee in ten minutes.'

Laura did as she was told.

She didn't sleep well that night and rose earlier than ever for her swim next morning. She needed to get rid of the demons that plagued her—perhaps exercise would do it.

There was someone else in the water when she got to the pool. She saw the swirl of white body and red trunks, performing an expert racing turn at the far end.

Showy, she thought to herself as she dived in. She didn't start her usual gentle plod up and down the pool but started a fast, energetic crawl. The man didn't interfere with her, and she was soon lost, happy in the forceful movement of her limbs against the water's buoyancy.

She'd almost forgotten the man's presence when there was a splash next to her as a head broke through from underwater. 'This is nice,' a voice said. She turned her head to see John's smiling face just a yard from her own.

'What are you doing—?' she started to say, and gulped down a mouthful of chlorinated water.

He'd taken her completely by surprise. She had to stop swimming and coughed desperately. A firm hand held her arm and lifted her half out of the water. 'This is what we do to children who are choking,' John's amused voice said, and he slapped her back. 'Or I can put my arms right round you and try the Heimlich manoeuvre.'

'Oof,' she spluttered, spraying water. 'I've swallowed half the pool and it's all your fault. And keep your arms to yourself.'

'Sorry,' he said amiably. 'I didn't mean to startle you.'

'Well, you did.' Her breathing was now returning to normal. She became conscious that they were standing in the shallow end of the pool close together and his arm was still around her. They were both nearly naked, and through the coolness of the water she could feel the pressure of his body against her leg, her hip, the curve of her breast.

'Anyway, what are you doing here?' she asked, moving away rather reluctantly.

He shrugged. 'I used to swim a lot. I just felt like the exercise.' He looked at her closely, water dripping from his long dark hair. 'You were putting a lot into it. Quite tired me to look at you.'

'I needed to.'

'Bad night?' he guessed. 'Your brother not coping too well?'

'Something like that.' She became even more aware of their bodies so close together. 'Look, I've got to do another five lengths.'

'I'll swim with you if you promise not to go too fast.'

She swam breaststroke now, with him at her side.

'You're having to support your family as well, aren't you?' he asked after a while.

Why should she lie? 'Something like that. There's never been any illness among them. They're not sure what to do.'

'But you're a medical person so they can lean on you. It's a burden, Laura.'

Fiercely she said, 'It's not a burden. They're my family and I love them.'

'It's when you love someone that the burden of illness gets harder. Now, I calculate that's your last five lengths.'

They both grasped the rail at the end of the pool. With a powerful kick and heave of his arms John pulled himself out of the water. Then he turned and offered her a hand.

It would have been childish and discourteous to ignore him. She took his hand and he pulled her easily onto the side.

She felt at a disadvantage. Her costume was a conservative one, designed for swimming not lying on a beach, but, still, he could see the curve and swell of her waist and breasts, the long length of her naked legs. She wished for the protection of her nurse's uniform, but there was also the thrill of knowing what effect her body was having on him. She could see the admiration burning in his eyes.

It was also the first time she had seen him looking so shockingly male. She realised that the flannels and dark shirts he usually wore with his white coat were a kind of camouflage. They made him seem comfortable, approachable, whereas this lean and muscled man was anything but comfortable. His sheer masculinity was breathtaking. She gazed at his wet form, at the thin line of dark hair that disappeared into the briefest of trunks. It was a new and entirely unsettling John.

'I'm on duty soon. I must go and change,' she said.

'Well, I'll do another dozen lengths. Just one thing, Laura. There'll be a message waiting for you on the ward. We've got a meeting this afternoon with the CE. He's moved fast on this trip to America.'

She had almost forgotten about it. How busy could she get? 'Good news?' she asked.

'Apparently. They've picked the ten children who are to go, and we're going to have our photographs taken for publicity.'

'I don't want publicity,' she wailed.

'We can't have everything we want,' he said smugly, 'I mean, look at me. You know what I want.'

Before she could guess what he was going to do he had bent his head and kissed her lightly on the mouth.

Their two cool, wet, near-naked bodies touched for an instant. She didn't know what to make of the flare of excitement it lit in her. 'You taste of swimming bath,' she accused him, wildly searching for something to say that would hide her agitation.

'And you taste delightful.'

He turned and dived in the same movement. For a moment she watched his body, cleaving the water, then she went to get changed.

The meeting that afternoon didn't take long. Laura had been specifically asked to come in her uniform. Before she was allowed to leave the ward a team of nurses had brushed her down, re-done her hair and critically assessed the minimal make-up she usually wore. John arrived, looking unusually urbane in a dark suit and hospital tie. Mark Black and David Miller went through the arrangements made so far, and then Harry Roscoe turned up.

After a couple of minutes' casual chat a reporter and photographer from the local paper were shown in. Dr Black said firmly that he would answer all questions, for which Laura was extremely grateful. Then there were the photographs—posing with John, shaking hands with Harry Roscoe, in a group of all of them. She hoped she didn't look too glassy-eyed.

It was only after the business was over, and they were drinking coffee together, that she was able to steal a couple of words with Harry Roscoe.

'I'd like to add my personal thanks for what you've done, Mr Roscoe,' she said. 'I really am most grateful.'

'You're welcome. And, I told you, I'm Harry and you're Laura.' He smiled benignly.

'That's nice…er, Harry. There's just one thing. Why did you insist on Dr Hawke and myself? There's a lot of other people who're probably better qualified than us for the job.'

'Ah. You're a sister in charge of a ward, Laura. Tell me, what makes one ward a happy, efficient place and another similar ward a living disaster?'

There was only one possible answer. 'A good, dedicated staff,' she said.

'Quite so. I've built up a successful business by picking the right people. And I'm sure I'm doing the right thing by picking you and John.'

'But you hardly know us!'

'I know you well enough,' he replied enigmatically. 'Perhaps I know you better than you know yourselves. Anyway, I've every confidence in my investment.'

CHAPTER SEVEN

'YOU look really nice,' Sal said over the phone, 'but I wish you'd let me have a go at your hair. I could have made you look knock-out.'

'Nurses in uniform aren't supposed to look knock-out,' Laura said. 'They're supposed to look smart or efficient or caring.'

Sal snorted. 'They're not supposed to look frumpish.'

Both of them had a copy of the local paper in front of them. On page five there was quite a long article and the pictures taken at the hospital. Laura had to admit she did look quite nice.

'Who's the man who's going with you?' Sal went on. 'He looks quite dishy to me.'

'His name's John Hawke and he's a doctor. In fact, he's the man who looked after Robert at the match.'

There was silence at the other end of the line for a moment, and then Sal said interestedly, 'I thought he was rather good-looking. I don't suppose you're—'

'No, I'm not,' Laura interrupted, 'but when I do you'll be the first to know.'

'Just trying to arrange another wedding,' said the unrepentant Sal. 'I'm going to write to the newspaper and order a copy of the picture of you. Will we be seeing you this afternoon?'

'Well, you know I'm on the ward right now and I'm working through. I'll see you tonight when you visit Robert. Bye, Sal.'

A few of her friends had already heard about the trip

123

to America. Now it had been in the newspaper it seemed that everyone in the hospital knew. She had collected all sorts of cheerful, semi-envious comments, but to her slight surprise most people seemed to think that she was the obvious person to go. 'I don't mind you holidaying in America,' one nurse had remarked, 'but I think it's a bit mean to take the hospital's prime unmarried man with you.'

'It's not like that,' Laura had protested, but she knew her task was hopeless.

Neither she nor John had to bother themselves with the arrangements for the trip. As he had promised, Dr Black organised nearly everything, working in tandem with Harry Roscoe. The two men were getting on well together. She was consulted only when it was necessary but had to deal with none of the petty but important details.

It was Saturday mid-morning and the ward for once was quiet. Laura allowed her thoughts to drift from work to her private life. So much had happened to her over the past few days that she'd coped by ignoring it. There had been the trauma of Robert's accident and the nagging worry of how he would cope. There was the trip to America. The furthest abroad she'd been so far had been to Ibiza. And last, and most important, was John Hawke. She liked him—she'd never met a man she liked more. He had turned her life upside down.

She sighed ruefully. Life at the moment was too complex. She wasn't sure where her relationship with John was going. She was still getting used to the idea that she was free of the emotional strait-jacket she'd fastened herself into. Like a good doctor, John was giving her time to recover but by now she should be able to act for herself. How?

Her phone rang, and she had a part answer.

It was Dr Black. There were a few personal details he required that she was able to provide at once. 'I don't suppose you know where Dr Hawke is, do you?' he went on. 'I'd really like to get this finalised today.'

She did know. 'He has the weekend off. He told me he had work to do at home and he intended to concentrate on it. He was even going to unplug his phone.'

'I wish I dared do that.' The CE sighed. 'Oh, well, it'll have to wait till Monday.'

She knew it was an offer she shouldn't make—but she made it. 'I finish work in an hour. If you like, I could walk across the park to his flat. If he's in I'll ask him to call you.'

'Would you? It would really simplify my weekend.'

She replaced the receiver, trying to pretend to herself that she didn't know why she'd volunteered. She'd hardly seen him for five days.

It had always seemed a bit unfair to Laura that not only did most diabetics have to inject themselves, they also had to test their own blood—sometimes two or three times a day. Surprisingly, most of them had no problem with pricking their fingers, and she had never come across a case of the pricking leading to an infection.

She had a few minutes to spare so she decided to use them to coach Natalie Platt. She called the girl into her office. 'Tell me about diabetes, Natalie.'

Natalie was nervous, but she'd been trained to deal with it. She shut her eyes, took a couple of deep breaths and said, 'Diabetes is a condition in which the body cannot use sugar and starches in the diet because the pancreas does not produce enough insulin. In 1921 Banting and Best discovered insulin in Toronto and...'

Laura let Natalie carry on with her account. It was

accurate and well learned, and when questioned Natalie showed that she understood her facts as well as she remembered them. The trouble was that they were still book-learned facts. Natalie needed more time on the wards.

'So why do we need to test for sugar, by using blood?' Laura broke in.

The answer was prompt. 'Testing the blood gives an immediate result. Testing urine is not as accurate.'

'Good. How does a patient test his or her blood?'

'By using a meter or by using a blood test strip.'

'What should you do before permitting an adult to start to test his own blood, using a strip?'

Natalie looked confused and Laura took pity on her. 'It's an unfair question but, remember, twenty per cent of men may be green/red colour blind. You must make sure your patient can read the colours on the strip accurately.'

'I see,' said Natalie. 'I hadn't thought of that.'

Laura took her onto the ward and showed her one of the techniques for testing blood. Nine-year-old Alice wriggled with importance as Laura told her that she was helping. 'You have to wash my hands first,' she told Natalie.

Under direction Natalie carefully pricked Alice's finger and squeezed till there was a large drop of suspended blood. She took a tube of strips, pulled one out, covered both pads on the test strip and timed the exposure for exactly sixty seconds. Then the strip had to be carefully wiped and there was another wait.

'Now check the colours on the two pads against the colours printed on the tube.'

Natalie did so, and read off Alice's blood glucose level. 'Why, it's easy,' she said.

*   *   *

The leaves were falling in the park now and there was a chill to the air. For a moment Laura allowed herself to look forward to the trip to America. They were going to Florida and Texas, and had been told it would be warm in both places. It should be interesting, especially as she was going with John.

Volunteering to go to John's flat was some kind of commitment, she realised. She wouldn't have done it before she'd found out the truth about Eric Myers. She wouldn't have been capable of it.

The previous two occasions on which she'd been to his flat had both been traumatic. He'd brought her here after Robert had been injured and again to meet Eric. The two visits had shown different sides of his character. There was the kind, thoughtful, sympathetic doctor and there was the tough-minded man who was willing to gamble that what he was doing was right. She wasn't sure which side was dominant.

His flat looked very attractive as she neared it. She could see the balcony with plants in pots, and she liked the deep red curtains. Just for a moment she wondered again if she should keep herself closeted in her tiny room in the nurses' home. She'd saved much of her salary and could easily afford to buy a small place of her own. Then she could entertain more. That was a new idea. She pressed button for John's flat.

'Hello?' A voice sounded from the intercom. Laura blinked. The voice was female.

Swallowing, she said, 'Er, this is Sister McLeod. I wanted to see Dr Hawke.'

'It's Laura, isn't it? Come on up—he's here. We're on the top floor.' It was a warm, friendly voice. A buzzer sounded and the door opened automatically. She stepped forward into the lobby.

She hadn't expected this. She'd come to deliver a message to John, not speak to some strange woman. For a moment she considered turning and walking away. Then, angry at herself, she headed for the stairs. Why shouldn't he entertain women if he wanted? After all, she had men friends.

She walked to the top floor. The flats were well kept, and there was expensive carpeting on the floors and plants on the window-ledges and by the side of the doors. As she climbed she realised that the woman had called her Laura. As they never had met that meant that John must have talked about her. She wasn't sure if she liked that.

Finally she reached his door. It opened as she approached it.

The woman was slightly taller than Laura and perhaps ten years older. Nearer John's age than her own. She was dressed in a tan suit that probably cost Laura's salary for a month, and her hair and make-up were equally impeccable.

'You must be Laura. I'm Gaynor Gladstone. I've heard such a lot about you.' Laura shook the outstretched hand, a little fazed by this obviously genuine friendliness.

'I shouted that it was you—he's here somewhere. Come on in.'

Laura entered. On the floor was a leather overnight bag, with a camelhair coat dropped carelessly on it.

Then a door closed at the far end of the hall and John appeared, shrugging into a jacket. Laura noticed his swift assessing glance at the two women. 'Laura?' he asked. 'Is everything all right?'

She thought he looked troubled, and she didn't like it.

He'd said he had work to do at home, she thought bitterly, and decided to leave at once.

'Sorry to bother you,' she said through gritted teeth, 'especially as you're busy, but the CE would like you to phone him. Nothing really important.'

She moved towards the door, and John hastened forward. 'Don't go yet, Laura. There's something I've got to show you. In fact, I was going to phone you later on.'

'You were? You have something to show me?'

'Something that will interest you. Now, I've just got to run Gaynor to the station—'

'Why doesn't Laura come too?' Gaynor interrupted. She turned to Laura. 'I don't want to go yet but there's only one through train in the next four hours. We can chat in the car.'

'All right,' Laura said faintly, 'I'll come with you.'

Gaynor put on the camelhair coat and John picked up her small bag. She must have stayed the night, Laura thought, and was pierced by another stab of jealousy.

Gaynor insisted that the two women sat in the back together. As soon as the car drew away she leaned forward and peered at Laura's face. It was an odd, detached scrutiny but for some reason it didn't make Laura feel uneasy.

'Hmm,' Gaynor muttered. 'Bones are very good, and I like the eyes. The hair's perhaps a bit too severe but we can easily alter that.' She pursed her lips and lifted Laura's plait. 'Voice might need a bit of work, but not much...not much at all.'

'My figure's quite good, too,' Laura said tartly, and was taken aback when Gaynor took her quite seriously.

'It is, indeed. We find that—'

'Gaynor, leave Laura alone,' John called from the

front with some exasperation. 'She's a nurse and a good one and she's going to stay that way.'

'And you're a good doctor,' Gaynor returned. 'That's why I want the pair of you. Your sincerity shows.'

Laura didn't know if she was angry or bewildered. 'Will someone please explain to me what's going on?' she demanded. 'I'm here. Don't talk about me—talk to me.'

Gaynor looked surprised, then realisation flooded her eyes. 'Oh, dear,' she said, 'I forgot. I've seen so much of you recently that I feel I know you. I'm so sorry.'

'You've seen so much of me?' Laura thought the conversation was now quite surreal.

In the front John roared with laughter. 'Laura, it's a bit late for introductions—but this is Gaynor Gladstone, Executive Producer of Gladstone films. She's an old friend of mine. She knows your face because for the past week she's been editing the film you helped to make about paediatric diabetes. You remember it?'

Laura did remember. She remembered very well.

'At the moment it's still a shoestring operation,' Gaynor said. 'I've only got a small contract at present, but a couple of big firms are interested in what I'm trying to do. There's a future for this kind of training video, Laura. And I'm going to be part of it.'

For a moment Laura saw a driven quality in her. She'd seen it before in doctors. John had a touch of it. It was a determination to get things right, get things done. Sometimes it could lead to an inability to see all sides of a question. Sometimes it could lead to obsession.

'You're quite good on film,' Gaynor went on. 'Not a natural like John, but I'm sure we could develop you. I'd like to use you.'

'I'm a nurse, not a film star,' Laura said. She decided that she didn't like the word 'use'.

'Why don't you leave talking to Laura to me?' John asked, and Gaynor seemed happy with that.

They pulled up in the station forecourt and John came round to open the door for Gaynor. 'You know how I feel about goodbyes,' she said. 'I have a ticket and a seat reservation. You're not to come on the platform with me. Hope to see you again, Laura.'

She turned to John. 'I've missed you.' Laura watched as she put her arms around him and kissed him full on the mouth. Then she turned away. There was a knowingness about Gaynor's actions that suggested that she and John were—or had been—more than just good friends. Why did it hurt so much?

John and Laura watched Gaynor stride purposefully away. 'She won't look back now,' John said. 'She's said goodbye and that's it.' Laura decided that the note in his voice was reluctant admiration rather than wistfulness. The figure turned into the station and was gone.

He asked Laura to sit in the front of the car with him and for a moment she was tempted to refuse, but that would have been childish so she sat by his side. When she saw the half-smile on his face she was more irritated than ever. He knew what she'd been thinking.

'I'd prefer it if you dropped me at the nurses' home,' she said, 'or I'll walk through the park. I've delivered my message.'

'So you have. But I want you to see the video you helped to make. And I thought perhaps we could sit and chat.' He glanced at the car clock. 'It'll soon be time for tea. I do these magnificent pizzas. All you need is a telephone and a ten-pound note.'

In spite of herself, Laura laughed. 'All right, I'll come,

but no pizza this time—I'm meeting Sal at half past four. Now, tell me about Gaynor. You once told me that there had been quite a long relationship in your life, and that you'd parted because the woman couldn't give you what you wanted. But you'd parted quite amicably. Was that woman Gaynor?'

'Yes,' he said, 'it was Gaynor.'

'I quite liked her,' Laura said. 'Did she just drop in casually?'

'Gaynor never does anything casually. She phoned early Friday evening, asking if she could come and stay. We had to talk about the video and she's trying to interest me in working with her on more of them.'

Laura sat silently for perhaps five minutes. Then it struck her. Because she hadn't asked questions once before she had jumped to a completely wrong conclusion. She would learn from previous mistakes.

'I have to ask,' she said painfully, 'but you don't have to answer if you don't want to. Are you thinking…that is, do you want…do you think you might get together again?'

He didn't reply at once, and her heart froze. Then he said seriously, 'I was very fond of Gaynor. In fact, I still am. I thought I was in love with her. But she wanted a career rather than children, and told me that wherever her career led she'd expect me to follow. Incidentally, she also saw me as helping her career. I was to have quite an important part in her videos. But I wanted a medical life of my own.'

'And you were never tempted?'

He paused again. 'Yes, I was tempted. But I now realise…I made the right decision.'

'You seemed very friendly.'

'We still are friends, but nothing more, Laura. We

couldn't be lovers again because...' His voice trailed away.

'Because?' she prompted.

'Because I've now realised that there's a difference between affection and love. I can now conceive of a relationship that's far more fulfilling than anything I could have with Gaynor. And that's what I want.'

'Are you talking about me?' she asked in a small voice.

'You know I am. We'll give it time—but not too much.'

She struggled to speak. 'At the moment I—'

He patted her arm. 'I know. Your feelings are tied up in all sorts of things. But I won't wait too long.'

'And are you going to work for Gaynor?'

He shook his head. 'I doubt it. Certainly I'll help her. I think the videos are a very worthwhile project. But I've already chosen my career.'

'I'm glad,' Laura said.

There was a companionable silence for a while. Then John switched on the car's stereo system and there was Frank Sinatra singing *Songs for Swinging Lovers*.

'D'you like Frank Sinatra?' she asked, rather surprised.

He turned and winked at her. 'Mood music,' he said, and she had to laugh. It was good that they could joke together.

'Sit there,' he said, waving her to a large, squashy chair when they were back in the flat, 'and don't say anything until the show is over. I'm going to phone Dr Black.' He clicked the remote control at the large screen.

A GLADSTONE MEDICAL TRAINING FILM was the title that flashed up. There was cheerful music, assorted cred-

its and then a view of a hospital ward. It was probably
a children's ward as there were large pictures on the
wall. The camera tracked down the centre of the ward
towards a white-coated figure, bending over a bed. Then
the figure stood, faced the camera and said, 'Hi, you've
just been told you've got diabetes. And you're not very
happy about it.'

Laura gaped at the picture as the figure went on,
'Well, I'm Dr John Hawke, and I want to explain things
to you.'

Her ward had lots of visual aids to stimulate the children—posters, strip cartoons, figures painted on the
walls. She had even seen one or two training videos, but
she'd never seen anything like this. With John as a com-
mentator, the film went through four case studies, inter-
viewing children and showing how they now lived useful and fulfilling lives. Her small part was shown here.
Then there was a scientific explanation of diabetes, with
cartoon characters jumping around an imaginary liver
and blood vessels. Last of all, John came back with a
gentle warning about the necessity of always being sure
you were doing the right thing.

Her own little speech didn't take up much time, but
she thought she'd done quite well and a vague feeling
of pride swelled inside her.

Two things made the video a good one. One was the
script—which was witty and amusing, but which covered all the necessary points. The other was the character
of John himself. Somehow he came over on screen just
as he appeared on the ward.

'John, that was brilliant,' she said sincerely when the
video was over. 'I've never seen anything half as good.
When did you make the rest of it?'

'I didn't make it—Gaynor did. There's an awful lot

that goes into something like that. I just presented it—Oh, and I wrote the script. A lot of the work was done when I was down in London.'

Laura was more impressed than ever but now she had further questions and somehow she didn't know quite how to phrase them. How could he work with Gaynor again?

John, however, wanted to talk about something else. 'How's your brother?' he asked. 'I know he's out of danger but...'

She winced. 'He's not good. Now he's over the worst of the operation he can see what comes next—a life in a wheelchair. And I don't think he can cope with it.'

John's eyes lit up with sympathy. 'I remember what it's like,' he muttered, 'that is...'

She'd already seized on what he'd said. 'You remember what it's like? How can you?'

He looked at her warily. 'Nothing much escapes you, does it, Sister McLeod? Yes, when I was at school I was knocked over by some idiot drunkard in a car. Broke my left leg and had a comminuted fracture of the right patella. I saw the X-rays some years later—there were bits of bone all over. Fortunately, I got a really good orthopaedic surgeon who managed to fit me together again but for a while there was a suggestion that I might be permanently crippled. As it was, I had to live in a wheelchair for a month.'

'You stayed at your boarding school?'

'There was an uncle in London who was my personal guardian, but I didn't want to stay with him and I don't think he wanted it either. I persuaded him not to let my parents know.'

'So you know what living in a wheelchair is like?'

'Yes. The little things irritate as much as the big ones.

But afterwards I had physio and I made a complete recovery. Probably that's where I got my first enthusiasm
for medicine.'

'I see. Being enthusiastic is one of the things I like
about you.'

'One of things? You mean there are more than one?'
he teased.

'You know what I mean,' she said primly. 'I like you
a lot, you've done things to help me and I find you…'

Suddenly the atmosphere in the room had changed.
No longer were they colleagues or friends, chatting casually. He moved from the couch where he was sitting
and knelt by her chair. Gently, oh, so gently, he stroked
her arm and shoulder. His touch was magic. She didn't
know whether she was calmed or excited. All she knew
was that she wanted him to do it more.

For a while she lay back, passive but happy under his
caresses. Her eyes closed. She sensed him moving and
she caught the faintest scent of his maleness. She knew
he was stooping over her. His hands cradled her face,
his fingertips touching her from her temple to the
warmth and the pulse of her neck. Her lips parted as his
brushed hers, soft and tentative as a butterfly on a flower.

It was lovely but it wasn't enough. Her arms wrapped
themselves around his neck, pulling her to him so their
bodies were pressed close together in the chair. His kiss
became more passionate, more demanding.

Inside Laura felt something stirring, a hunger for him
and a knowledge that now she could give himself to him.
She was her own woman, and her soul or her heart were
hers to bestow how she wished. The feeling of exhilar-
ation was so great that she wanted to cry with joy.

He moved away, and she was desolate. 'John?' she
asked.

His reply was prosaic but it jolted her back to reality. 'It's twenty past four. You're meeting Sal in ten minutes.'

'I must go!' Sal still couldn't bear to see her son without Laura's comforting presence. If Laura wasn't there she'd fret and worry.

'I'll run you back.' They both stood. Suddenly his arms were around her and he kissed her again. 'We've started something, Laura, you know that.'

'I know it. And I like it.'

CHAPTER EIGHT

LAURA loved America. It was warm, it was friendly, it was different. There was hardly any work for her to do—she felt at times that she was there under false pretences.

And she was with John. When she saw him for the first time each morning her heart gave a little bounce. When she was with him during the day she was content. And she could tell that he was getting even fonder of her. It showed in his eyes, in the way he treated her during the day. But for the moment they were at work, not on holiday together. Any decisions could wait.

Having had experience of organising trips, she had been amazed at how smoothly things had gone. She and John had been consulted only on essential matters—basically the medication and care of the ten nine- to fourteen-year-olds they'd taken.

She knew them all, of course. She had been particularly pleased that Brian Hughes had come—she'd felt he'd needed a holiday. Then there was Barry Brent, much happier now he'd been placed with a foster-family. Alice Trenton was the smallest and youngest, and sometimes had seemed to be the one who'd made most noise.

Mary Walsh was the oldest girl, aged fourteen but contriving to look nineteen. Laura had looked at her deep red lipstick, eye-shadow and mascara, and had felt decidedly old-maidish. In spite of suggestions about dress for the flight, Mary had worn the shortest, tightest miniskirt imaginable. I'm going to have to watch you, Laura had thought, then had felt slightly ashamed at being a spoilsport. Mary was always ready to help with the younger children.

There had been more publicity photographs at the airport. Harry had provided everyone with a flight bag, two T-shirts and a sweater, each coloured bright blue and with ROSCOE TRAVEL SERVICE emblazoned across the front. Firmly pinned to each sweater was a name-tag.

'They'll make the kids easier to spot,' Harry shrewdly pointed out. 'In a place like The Magic Kingdom that's quite an advantage. And if you wear them the kids can see you.'

'I'm beginning to see why you've made such a lot of money,' she said. 'It's attention to detail, isn't it?'

He winked at her. 'Partly. And the rest is employing good staff.'

Then there were the last goodbyes to supervise and the occasionally tearful kiss—from the parents rather than the children.

There was a moment's excitement when Mary's pen-injector showed up on the X-ray machine and she had to take it out and proved it wasn't a weapon. The inspector blinked when he saw John's bag, full of ampoules and syringes, but Harry had already explained the particular circumstances. Then they were on their way, standing in a colourful line on the moving walkway that took them to their final departure gate.

All the children had spent the previous night at the hospital—and a feverishly excited night it had been too. With their breakfasts they had all taken travel sickness pills—they would calm them and with any luck there'd be no problems on the flight. They filed docilely onto the plane and took their seats.

For take-off Laura and John had decided to sit apart so they could keep an eye on the children. But there was no need. There was more fear shown by some of the adults than their charges. When the seat-belt sign flashed off she went to sit next to him.

'Exciting, isn't it?' he greeted her. 'No matter how many plane trips I take, I still love that first leap into the air.'

She was surprised. 'I would have thought an old sophisticate like you would be used to flying by now. Complaining about the food and having no leg room.'

'I'm just a little boy at heart. Did you know Harry's arranged for a couple of the older ones to have a look in the cockpit later? Well, I'm going to go, too.'

'If you're not too busy.'

There were things for them to see to during the flight. Laura kept a wary eye on the meals served and suggested that some things should be left. Fortunately there were plenty of carbohydrates. She also wanted to make sure that no one thought that this was a special occasion, and that they might just once over-indulge in sugar-filled drinks.

There were the headphones to sort out so they could watch the in-flight film and each of the younger children had to be accompanied to the toilet for the first time, but things seemed to go smoothly.

The children had all had an injection at breakfast-time. John had calculated that they wouldn't need one on the flight. However, Laura tested the smaller children for blood sugar, just to be sure.

After three hours a cabin attendant bent over John and whispered, 'Dr Hawke? I think we have a bit of an emergency with a lady in Club Class. It could be a…it looks to me like a heart attack. Do you think you and the nurse could…?

He raised his eyebrows at Laura and they followed

the attendant down the plane. 'This is Mrs Canning,' she said. 'Mrs Canning, dear, here's a doctor and a nurse.' Then she stood well back.

The attendant had reclined the seat and Mrs Canning, an overweight lady of about sixty, looked up at John imploringly. 'It's my heart,' she gasped. 'It feels like I'm going to die. And the pill didn't work. You've got to do something, Doctor.'

Laura noticed her pale skin and the beads of perspiration on Mrs Canning's forehead.

John took hold of his patient's wrist. 'You've had this trouble before?' he queried.

'It's angina worse than it's ever been. The pain's spread across my chest and down my left arm. I've got these pills and if I have an attack I put one under my tongue. They've always made me feel better but it didn't work today. I must be having a real heart attack.'

'I don't think we need worry too much yet,' John said soothingly. 'The stress of flying often makes people feel worse than they really are. Now, where are your tablets, Mrs Canning?'

'In my handbag.'

John nodded to Laura who pulled the handbag from beneath Mrs Canning's feet and opened it. Inside was a foil-topped phial. She handed it to John.

She knew, of course, about angina pectoris, though she seldom came across it in a children's ward. The coronary arteries hardened and could cause great pain if the sufferer exerted him- or herself or ate too much or was subject to an emotional shock—like fear of flying. The treatment was to take a vasodilator, which relaxed the constricting walls of the arteries. However, this time the vasodilator didn't seem to have worked. For a moment Laura had visions of this being a real emergency and of

the plane having to make an emergency landing somewhere. But they were over the middle of the Atlantic!

John seemed to be puzzled too. He looked at the phial
and muttered. 'The usual glyceryl trinitrate. It should
have worked.' He opened the bottle and tipped out the
contents. There were only a few left.

Suddenly he smiled and looked at the outside of the
phial again. He smile grew broader. 'There are only a
few here, Mrs Canning. Do you have a new supply
somewhere?' he asked.

'In my flight bag. The pink leather one.'

This time Laura reached to the overhead locker to get
the bag. Inside was an ornate wash-bag containing an
alarming number of preparations, including an unopened
phial of glyceryl trinitrate.

John took the phial, cracked the opening and shook
out a pill. 'Try this one, Mrs Canning,' he said.

'But I've just—'

'It's all right. This one will work.'

Mrs Canning put the pill under her tongue as directed.
John turned to Laura and winked. 'I think the emergency
is over now, Nurse,' he said. 'Why don't you go back
to your seat?'

'Of course, Doctor,' she said sarcastically, and did as
she was told. She was still mystified, though.

Fifteen minutes later he slipped back into his seat next
to her. 'Mrs Canning is feeling much better,' he said.
'The panic is over.'

Laura couldn't contain herself. 'Why are you so sure?
And why didn't the first pill work?'

He smiled. 'I looked at the date they were issued.
Over three months ago. If she opened them at once, by
now they'll be going off. Glyceryl trinitrate only lasts
about eight weeks once it's exposed to the air.'

'I see,' said Laura. 'Did you tell her what had happened?'

'I did. She said her GP had warned her, but she'd forgotten.'

'Hmm.' Laura had never been really ill, but she was always surprised at the casual way some people treated their doctor's advice and instructions. 'Forgotten, indeed,' she said.

'I'll go back in half an hour and see how she's getting on.' John reached for his book.

Ten minutes later the attendant came back to them, carrying a tray with two glasses and a bottle of champagne. 'Captain Benlow's thanks,' she said, deftly pouring the wine. 'He says he didn't really want to turn back to Ireland. And would you accept this with the compliments of the airline?'

'It'll be a pleasure,' John said, handing a glass to Laura.

Otherwise, it was an uneventful flight. It seemed no time before they were flying down the American coastline, looking at great forests and then an apparently unending seaboard.

Time to land. The seat-belt sign flashed on and the scream of the jet engines altered. Then they were swooping down to a strangely foreign landscape, scattered with palm trees, bright green fields and numberless tiny lakes. Orlando, in Florida, home of Walt Disney World.

They were met by their two guides, Dwight Johnson and Helen Zwingli. Both were youngish, earnest and super-efficient. Laura had to stifle a laugh when she first saw them, and knew that John had the same reaction. Both guides were dressed in long shorts and Harry Roscoe

T-shirts. Dwight was tall, thin and blond. Helen was tall, thin and brunette. They both had the same short haircut.

'Good afternoon, ma'am, sir,' said Dwight. 'I hope you had a good flight. I'll go and attend to the baggage and Helen would like to familiarise herself with the children. I'll be back with the coach in fifteen minutes.'

He turned to the group now clustered around Helen and called, 'Hey, kids, I'm Dwight. See you soon, OK?'

'Shout back, "OK, Dwight,"' Helen urged. 'Come on, all together, "OK, Dwight!"'

John drew Laura aside to a seat. 'I've got an idea that we won't be doing too much this trip,' he said. 'As soon as they've finished familiarising themselves Helen and Dwight will have everything sewn up. Perhaps I can spend some time familiarising myself with you?'

'I don't think I like men who get familiar,' she said, and burst into giggles. 'But so far I like these two. They're enthusiasts, good at their job. They'd be good children's nurses.'

'That's praise, coming from you.' He stroked her arm, a quick gentle caress, and she shivered.

'Both Dwight and I are at college, majoring in tourism,' Helen explained when they were all safely aboard the small, air-conditioned coach. 'And we work for Mr Roscoe to get the money to pay for our course and to get experience.'

'Do you like working for him?' Laura asked.

'A very good employer, ma'am. You'd think he was an American.' It was obvious that Helen thought this was a supreme compliment. 'He expects good work but he pays well. You'll be asked to report on us and we welcome that. We just hope you'll tell us if there's any way we're falling short.'

'I don't think that's likely to happen,' Laura said sincerely.

Orlando was about half an hour's drive from the airport. While Dwight drove, Helen kept the children's attention, by pointing out places they might visit in the next few days. Then they pulled up at the motel where they were to stay.

'I think a quick meal and then an early night,' John muttered to Laura. 'Even though they all slept on the plane, the clock's gone back five hours. We'll examine them all before they go to sleep.'

'Sounds a good idea,' she said.

They had their own wing of the motel, with special semi-dormitory accommodation for the girls and boys. Helen and Dwight were to sleep with their charges, and John and Laura had their own rooms. After a specially arranged meal in the motel restaurant the children were brought one by one to John's room where he gave them a swift examination and checked their blood sugar. Laura injected the younger children and watched while the older children injected themselves. Nothing much was wrong.

'Remember,' John said to Helen and Dwight before they finally went to bed, 'if there's the slightest problem you're to come to get me. It doesn't matter what time of the night it is—I want to be told.'

'We'll certainly see to that, sir,' Helen said.

There was nothing more for Laura to do. Dwight and Helen were now firm favourites with their charges. John went with Dwight while Laura watched Helen, helping the girls get ready for bed, and decided she could be left to it. Harry Roscoe had triumphed again. These were good people. With a whispered goodnight she went to her own room.

She hadn't had a chance to look at it closely before. Now she walked around, admiring it. It was about four times the size of her room in the nurses' home. There were prints on the wall, a large television and an even larger bed. In the bathroom was a great pile of fluffy white towels.

She switched on the television and began to unpack, hanging her clothes in the more than generous wardrobe space. She hadn't brought much—in fact, she hadn't much to bring. Once again she wondered if her life was following the right path. She could easily afford to spend more money on clothes so why didn't she?

In spite of fierce pushing from Sal, she hadn't even bought herself a bikini. Her old black swimsuit would have to do. 'You're not going there to swim,' Sal had snapped. 'You're going to show that figure. As much of it as possible!'

'No, I'm not,' Laura had replied. 'I'm going to stay safe.' But now, in a luxurious room in a foreign city in a distant land, she wondered if staying safe was quite so wonderful.

'We'll stop for a beer, Lewis,' an English voice said behind her, and she turned to find that she wasn't so far from home. The television was showing the same English detective series that she'd watched last week, but the views of Oxford spires seemed distinctly out of place here.

Someone knocked on the door. Warily she opened it—and there was John, clutching two plastic cups. 'Not showering or in bed, are you?' he asked, and waited to be invited in.

'Not yet, but soon. I keep forgetting that it's really two o'clock in the morning. Come on in.'

He sat on her bed and offered her one of the cups. 'I

thought you might like something before you sleep. There's a little coffee-bar in Reception and I bought these two. See what you think.'

She took off the lid and smelled cautiously. It was a warm drink, dark in colour with an odd flowery scent. She sipped. It was…different. 'What is it?' she asked.

'It's blackberry tea. The Americans are very fond of fruit and herbal teas. I find them quite refreshing.'

She sipped again. He was right. It was a completely new taste to her but very pleasant. 'Do you always try new things in a foreign country?' she asked.

'If it's possible. There's a whole range of teas to try. I'll have cinnamon tomorrow. Doesn't do to get too set in your ways, Laura.'

She looked at him speculatively. 'Are you trying to tell me something?'

'Just inviting you to join me in a breakfast cup of cinnamon tea,' he said urbanely. 'Nothing more.'

'Hmm.' She drank again and discovered she liked it more with each mouthful. And she was sitting on a bed with a man she liked in a strange city. Suddenly she couldn't keep her eyes open. A great wave of tiredness hit her and she was only dimly aware that she'd slumped against John. She felt him take the half-empty cup from her hand and a comforting voice said, 'Well, I know I'm boring at times, but this is ridiculous. Bedtime, Laura. Are you capable of undressing yourself?'

That did make her stir. 'Certainly,' she said, as distinctly as she could. 'Just a bit tired after the flight. Good…goodnight, John.'

He put his arms around her. She was aware of his warmth and the vague masculine smell as he pulled her to him. He kissed her once on the cheek. 'Night, Laura. Go to bed.' Then he was gone.

Somehow she managed to pull herself upright, lock the door, turn off the television and clean her teeth. She had no energy for her usual bedtime routine. Her clothes stayed where they dropped. Then she was in bed, smiling to herself as she slept.

Laura awoke, wondering where she was. Then she remembered. She was in America! Her eyes flicked around the room, noting the rays of sunshine behind her thick curtains. There was a knock on the door—the second, she realised. Scrambling out of bed, she grabbed her dressing-gown and unlocked the door.

It was John again, this time clutching just one plastic cup. 'Your cinnamon tea, ma'am,' he said, offering her the cup. 'I trust you slept well?'

'Perfectly well, thank you,' she gabbled. 'I don't know what came over me last night.'

'You were just very tired.' With a wicked grin he waved behind her and said, 'That's not the super-tidy Nurse McLeod whom we all love.'

She turned. In a line leading from the bathroom were boots and socks, trousers, sweater, shirt and, most obviously, bra and briefs in a matching shade of light blue. 'Out!' she said, taking the cup from him. 'I'll be with you as soon as I've showered.'

The cinnamon tea was an experience, she supposed, but she doubted whether she'd want to repeat it. On the other hand, the shower was magnificent. The water pressure was only moderate at the top of the nurses' home. Here she felt as if she were standing under a warm waterfall. Ten minutes later she was outside, looking for John.

They'd left the chilly weather of near-winter behind. Here it was just warm enough to be comfortable and not in the least humid. She felt quite happy in her T-shirt and shorts.

John was similarly dressed, sitting in the sun by the pool. 'Come and sit for five minutes,' he said. 'Soon we start work.'

'Work?' she asked. 'On a day like—?'

'Hi,' a voice behind them said. 'Everyone's excited and ready to go. D'you want to check them out before breakfast?' It was Dwight, as efficient as ever.

John winked at Laura. 'We'll just have a quick look to see if there are any problems.' It was going to be a busy day.

Their first trip was to The Magic Kingdom. It had been decided to go to the most exciting places first. John and Laura were well aware that the younger children especially could easily get exhausted. Dwight drove them there in the bus and once inside they took the ferry across the Seven Seas Lagoon. Then they split into two groups, the older children going with John and Helen and the younger ones with Laura and Dwight. Dwight provided a map with the suitable rides marked. 'See you for lunch,' John called.

It was a good morning. The younger children visited Fantasyland first and then went to It's A Small World. Meanwhile, the older ones went straight to Tomorrowland and headed for the star ride—Space Mountain. There was far too much to see and do. By the end of the morning it was easy to see that the younger ones were flagging, and after their light lunch Laura said she'd sit with them to watch Disneymania.

They actually left quite early, to vociferous complaints from some of the older children. John and Laura had decided that the last thing they wanted was to overtire anyone. Dwight took them on a scenic ride around

Orlando and Helen helped them keep a log of all the birds they spotted.

The next day they went to Universal Studios and the day after that to the Disney/MGM Studios. Seeing how much Dwight and Helen were putting into their work, John insisted that they took the two evenings off. He and Laura could see to the children. In fact, there wasn't much to see to. At the end of each day the children were always exhausted.

The final trip was to Cape Canaveral. Fortunately there wasn't too much walking to do here, but the children were enthralled by the IMAX film show and the tour around the rocket site. Laura had never quite realised how vast rockets were and how tiny the living spaces perched on the ends. As they drove away, Dwight slowed the bus and pointed to something perched on the top of a telegraph pole. 'We're in luck, kids. See, there's a great bald eagle. It's the American national bird.'

Laura stared at the motionless creature. Behind it was swamp and then, in the distance, the gantries and rockets of the space station. She thought it was somehow symbolic of the United States.

Dwight and Helen insisted on being on duty that night so after their meal and the regular little medical inspection Laura felt her time was her own. After the day by the sea she felt grubby so she had a long shower and shampooed her hair. Then she decided she'd had enough of shorts and T-shirt for a while—comfortable though the outfit was. Instead, she rummaged through her wardrobe and took out a simple white dress. For a change she'd dress as a female, instead of wearing the unisex uniform they'd all adopted.

It was dark when she stepped out of her room but still warm. In front of her were the central grounds of the motel with carefully watered and manicured lawns, palm trees and the odd-shaped swimming pool, now illuminated from underneath. Sitting by the pool was John. He had heard her door snap shut, and turned and waved to her.

'How nice you look,' he said, rising as she joined him, 'I'd almost forgotten how attractive you were in a skirt.' He made a space for her to sit by him on his bench.

'My old English teacher said that using the word "nice" was an indication of an idle mind and a limited vocabulary,' Laura said cheerfully. 'She never got married—we all thought it was because she could never find a man who knew more words than she did.'

'It's one good reason for not getting married. I'll bet you were good at English, weren't you, Laura?'

Well, yes, she had been—but how had he guessed that? 'I like it,' she said. 'I still liked reading.'

'So do I. It's a pleasant—solitary—pastime.'

She felt uneasy. 'I don't do it because it's solitary— I do it because I like it.'

'What better reason is there? Anyway, come and sit here. You know, even in summer it's not often that you can sit out at this time of night in England. A pity, really.'

She sat by him. 'Palm trees, soft wind—even a moon,' she said. 'It's—'

'Romantic?'

'No. I was going to say very nice.'

She relaxed as they laughed together. It struck her again that she'd never met a man like John. He was so easy to be with, so much in tune with the way she thought. And yet there was another side to him—a determination that both attracted and slightly frightened her. As she looked at him she had to recognise that he was also one of the most physically attractive men she'd ever met.

He was the man for her, she was sure. The realisation came almost as a shock, then she knew she'd known it for weeks. Why had she taken so long to come to this realisation? And why here and now?

'I've got you a drink,' he said. 'I thought you might be thirsty after a day by the sea.' He offered her a tall glass.

Laura tried wildly to wrench her thoughts back to the ordinary world. Not that this world was ordinary. But she could hardly say that she'd just decided that she loved him.

'What is it?' she asked faintly.

'It's beer—American beer. I'm having the same myself.'

'I don't drink beer.' It was an automatic response. Some of the girls in the rugby club had drunk beer— even pints.

'This is different. It's iced, it's light and it's refreshing. Now, just try it—don't be influenced by preconceptions.' Gingerly she tried it. It wasn't too bad. She took another mouthful and decided she liked it. It was more refreshing than the extra-sweet drinks she'd been taking.

It was very pleasant to be sitting out here with John, the warm, softly scented breeze blowing around them. Five minutes earlier she'd been looking forward to a chance to unwind, to spend time with a man whose company she enjoyed. Now it was different. She was with a man she loved. But she couldn't tell him!

'It's good to relax,' John said. 'I've enjoyed things so far, but I think it's time to move on. The kids are getting a bit over-tired—they need the rest.'

If he only knew how unrelaxed she felt at that moment! 'Are you getting tired, too?' she managed to ask.

He thought for a moment. 'I suspect I'm the same as you. I've enjoyed everything we've done—but there's always the awareness that we are here as responsible adults. We can never entirely relax.' After a while he added, 'But it's peaceful now.'

'Yes, it is.'

'Are you all right, Laura? You seem a bit withdrawn.'

She couldn't talk yet. She needed time to make sense of her tumultuous thoughts. 'Such a lot has happened,' she said. 'It's all been so exciting. I suppose I'm still getting used to things.'

'It's a voyage of discovery. For us as well as the kids.' Somehow he knew what she was thinking.

It seemed the most obvious thing in the world for him to move down the bench and put his arm around her shoulders. She sighed and leaned on him. No need to think now.

After a while he bent and kissed her. She closed her eyes and put her arms around him. When his kisses grew more demanding she didn't push him away. She wanted him—in all ways.

After a while, with infinite reluctance, he broke off. 'I was enjoying that,' she said mournfully. He took her hand, moved it under his T-shirt and held it against his chest. She could feel his warmth and the beat of his heart. 'It's fast,' she said.

'Do you know why?'

As reply she took his hand and slid it under her own shirt. It was an act that surprised even her. She'd never been so forward with a man before. It was exciting to feel his fingers curve round her ribs, his thumb brushing her bra. 'I know why,' she said softly, 'because my heart is the same. You know, I think I'm—'

'Dr Hawke? Oh, Dr Hawke?' It was Dwight's voice, and even as John slowly moved his hand he wryly recognised the thoughtfulness with which he had called, before disturbing them.

'Is there a problem?' John asked calmly as Dwight arrived.

'Possibly, sir, possibly. Everyone's fine except young Gareth, and he's having difficulty in getting to sleep. I've felt his forehead and he seems a little heated to me. Would you mind having a look?'

'Of course.' John stood. 'This shouldn't take too long, Laura. Do you want to wait up and we'll have a last drink?'

But the easy, relaxed mood had gone, and she remembered they were here to work. 'I'm feeling quite tired. I think I'll go to bed,' she said hesitantly. 'Today's been…quite exciting. I need time to think. But if you need any nursing care don't hesitate to wake me.'

His face was in shadow and she couldn't see his expression, but his voice was calm enough. 'If I need any nursing care I'll wake you,' he said, and turned to follow Dwight.

She went to her room but she knew there was no way she would sleep. In desperation she had another shower, ignoring the fact that she'd had one not an hour previously. Then she got into bed, turned off the light and stared at the ceiling. She didn't want John to knock, thinking she was awake.

She was in love with John Hawke, but for so long she had been wary, for so long she had kept him at a distance, that she didn't quite know what to do now. She couldn't, just couldn't tell him that she was in love with him. It might have been easier if they had been on holiday alone, but they were here to work. And she wasn't sure she knew how to show him exactly how she felt. Habits of caution and restraint were hard to throw off.

After twenty minutes she heard soft voices from further down the wing of the motel, and the click of a door shutting. Then there was the pad of regular footsteps, getting louder as they came nearer. It was John. Under the sheet her body tensed. Did the steps slow as he approached her door? She wasn't sure. He didn't stop, and moments later she heard him open his own door. She could relax, perhaps go to sleep. But she didn't.

The next day they took things very easy. There had been nothing seriously wrong with Gareth, but John thought it was a sign that the children needed a break. In the morning they walked for a while in Leu Botanical Gardens then they returned to the motel and Laura helped Helen with the children's packing. They were starting the next stage of their holiday and Laura was looking forward to it with anticipation.

She had to say something to John. 'Sorry I went to bed so quickly last night,' she muttered, 'but I was tired.'

'No problem,' he said blandly. 'I was quite enjoying our talk. We'll take it up again soon.'

She looked at him, disturbed. Could he have guessed the sudden revelations she'd had? 'I...enjoy being with you,' she said. It wasn't much of a declaration but it was a start.

'And I love being with you.' He reached over and ran his hand down her naked arm, one of the frequent gentle caresses that she found so exciting. 'Now, is everyone packed?' Time to work again.

The next stage of their trip was something quite new.

They were going to travel from Orlando to El Paso in Texas by train. Laura traced the journey on a map and checked the mileage. It was over 1700 miles! England would fit into Texas!

Dwight and Helen were coming with them. Apparently, this was one of the trips that Harry often arranged. 'Travelling by Amtrak is a totally different experience from anything I know,' Dwight said. 'It's both restful and exciting.'

'That's a clever trick,' Laura murmured to herself.

They waited by the track on Orlando station. Unlike England, there was no platform. When the train came they would have to climb up to it. The children were getting excited. There was a soft moaning sound and down the track came the biggest train she had ever seen. It was enormous, two storeys high. Gracefully it pulled past them and came to a slow halt. She couldn't help comparing it with the bustle of an aeroplane.

They had places reserved at the rear of the train, a set of sleeping compartments with four berths that converted into seats during the day. For the two nights they'd be on the train there would be an adult sleeping in each compartment. She marvelled at the compactness of the compartments—and the comfort, too.

They settled in their seats and the train slowly drew out. Laura had always thought that there was more of the country to be seen from a train window than practically any other means of transport. Dusk slowly came on, and she peered into the backs of houses, down little town main streets, at long stretches of water-filled woodland.

The train didn't move very quickly and they seemed to stop every hour or two at some tiny, dimly lit station. The group went for a meal in the restaurant car and quickly returned to the sleeping cars. There was something hypnotic about the gently swaying carriages and the click of the rails outside. Everyone was tired, too. They all went to bed early.

Next morning Dwight and Helen fetched breakfast from the buffet car. After that everyone read, played games or just stared out of the window.

'Why are they all so lethargic?' Laura whispered to John.

'I'm not sure. Perhaps we've done too much too quickly. Whatever it is, I'm feeling it, too.' He squeezed her arm and left. On the train they were all thrown together, and there was no opportunity for a long private conversation. She was rather glad about that.

They pulled into New Orleans for a three-hour stop. It was raining, a hot steady rain. The four senior members conferred and decided there would be little point in taking the children off the train. Besides, none of them wanted to move. Only John went for a half-hour walk around the station.

They set off again through a long succession of flat, rural landscapes. Most of the children slept, and John looked at them approvingly.

By the second evening everyone was starting to come to life. After their evening meal Dwight and Helen took the children to watch a film in the downstairs buffet car, and John and Laura stayed upstairs in the observation lounge.

Laura loved the observation lounge. There were small tables and comfortable chairs facing the glass side of the carriage. From the little bar you could buy drinks, coffee and snacks. And outside was the slowly unfolding panorama of Texas. It was a big country.

John fetched her a beer. She'd decided she quite liked

it, though whether she'd continue drinking it back in England she wasn't sure. For a while they sat side by side, watching the countryside roll by. John was one of those people who didn't need conversation all the time, but could enjoy companionship in silence. He wasn't like Sal and her family—they always had to be chatting.

Shadows crept across the almost deserted lounge, and in the distance they could see the pinpricks of light from far-off farms. He reached over and took her hand. With a sense of inevitability she didn't try to stop him.

'Are you happy, Laura?' he asked. 'You still seem a bit preoccupied.'

'I'm very happy. I think I've come to a decision and it's just a bit frightening. We're moving miles across a continent towards somewhere exciting and a bit strange. And I feel I'm moving towards something as well.'

She looked at him, wondering if he'd understand. He did. 'I'm happy for you,' he said. 'And for me, too.'

CHAPTER NINE

THE train rumbled on through the night. They all slept well again, and next morning the landscape had changed. The green grass and cultivated fields had disappeared. Instead, there was the dark brown of semi-desert, and in the distance were ranges of high mountains.

The children changed, too. They had rested long enough and now they were growing restless, ready for exercise. Dwight and Helen did the best they could to keep them amused with games and stories, but everyone was now looking forward to their afternoon arrival.

'See those mountains,' Dwight said, pointing to a dark range that looked close enough to touch. 'Well, those mountains are in Mexico.' They were dropping out of the desert into El Paso. 'Cowboy-and-Indian country,' Helen said.

'Will we see any Indians?' asked nine-year-old Alice. 'Will they chase us?'

'I think we'll see some,' Helen said, 'but I don't think we'll get chased.'

It was good to leave the train and look forward to walking again. The weather had changed. The sun was out and it was quite warm, but there was no softness in the air as there had been in Florida. This was no country for lounging around. Laura felt invigorated.

Their baggage was taken into the big red-brick station. Waiting for them was a tall, bronzed man, with long raven-black hair tied in a ponytail. He was lean and dressed in a denim jacket. His jeans were held by a broad belt with a silver and turquoise inlays. 'Hi,' he said. 'My name's Jim Peyote. I'm to be your driver for the next few days.'

Alice pressed close to Laura's shirt. 'Are you an Indian?' she asked.

'I surely am. I'm a member of the Navajo nation.'

'Where's your feathered hat?'

'It's back in my hogan. That's where I live.'

'Are you going to shoot cowboys?'

Seriously, he shook his head. 'We don't shoot cowboys any more. Now, do you all want to get on the coach?'

Dwight and Helen had met Jim before and performed swift introductions. 'This is Jim's country,' Helen explained. 'He can show you things that we don't know about.'

'Harry Roscoe sends me quite a few parties,' Jim said. 'We don't get too many people coming from England.'

They drove swiftly out of the conurbation that was El Paso. Then they drove through a narrow mountain pass and soon they were crossing the desert. Jim had chosen a secondary road and there wasn't another vehicle for miles. After half an hour he pulled off into a layby and asked everyone to get out. 'You've all been in vehicles too long,' he said. 'Let's wander around a bit.'

'I like it here,' Laura murmured to John, who was standing next to her. 'Just smell the air. And the country's sort of big. There's plenty of space for everybody.'

He, too, drew in a deep breath. 'Just the place for kids with chest troubles,' he said practically. 'You could open a great TB sanatorium here.'

She elbowed him. 'You can indulge me for once. Let me be a romantic occasionally.'

'You can be romantic with me as often as you like,' he whispered, and she blushed.

Jim led the children off the road, down a shallow valley he called an arroyo. The adults followed at a distance. 'There's even room for the plants,' Laura went on. 'Look, plenty of bare ground—and every now and then something growing. Things aren't all crammed together like they are in England.'

Jim had stopped and the children gathered round him. 'My grandfather hunted for food with a bow and arrows,' he said. 'And to find food you have to track it. Now, what can you see here?'

They were staring at a patch of sand, blown smooth by the wind. Across it were a set of odd, curving lines. 'There are no hoof marks,' one of the older boys said tentatively, 'so it's not an animal.'

'Do all animals have hoofs?'

'It's the marks a snake makes,' someone else said.

'Right. Snakes can make good food. Now, how long is the snake?'

Laura had thought that at the first mention of a snake the children would panic, but Jim had enthralled them. He didn't bother so neither did they. After they'd looked at the snake marks they went further up the arroyo, and he showed them how to tell if a man was running or walking, how to estimate how tall and heavy he was and what happened if he fell over.

'Harry Roscoe strikes again,' John said to Laura as they watched the engrossed children. 'Jim Peyote is marvellous.'

They were to stay the first three nights in a chalet camp deep in New Mexico. As usual they were greeted with complete efficiency. After the children had a quick medical check, Dwight and Helen supervised the evening meal and then their bedtime routine. There was nothing for John and Laura to do. 'Let's go for a wander,' John said.

It was one of the occasional snatched times when she was alone with him, and which she valued so much. His hand grazed hers as they walked, and she wondered if she should take it and hold it.

Eventually they found themselves at the bottom of the camp, where there were benches around a barbecue pit. Jim Peyote was sitting on a bench. He raised a hand in greeting but didn't speak.

Jim and Laura sat, too. In front of them the desert stretched away to the far distance where mountains, now black against the setting sun, formed a saw-toothed border. The colours of the land were different, and because of the clearness of the air even distances seemed different. From the sun-warmed land came an arid scent like nothing they'd ever smelled before. It was all so empty.

John took her hand and she was at peace with the world. There was no need to speak—just being was enough.

Then she heard the crunch of feet behind her, not the light step of a child but the confident stride of an adult. She hoped it wasn't Helen or Dwight, bringing them a problem.

A voice said, 'Why, it's John—and Laura, too. How nice to see you both.' There was a moment of complete disbelief and then Laura's happiness collapsed in splinters around her. It was Gaynor Gladstone.

It was small consolation that John apparently felt the same.

'Gaynor! What are you doing here? How did you find us?' His voice was sharp.

'What a greeting! I found you by phoning the hospital and then faxing Harry Roscoe. I couldn't believe my luck when they said you were here in New Mexico. It's only a short plane ride from Los Angeles.' She came to sit on the other side of John. He'd let go of her hand, Laura noticed bitterly.

'Well, of course, it's very nice to see you,' John said. Laura realised he'd regained his usual calmness. 'But is this just a social call?'

'No. John, I've got *the* job for you. I've landed the contract I've always dreamed of—a complete medical series, funded by one of the biggest medical foundations on the coast. And I want you to be chief medical advisor and presenter.' She lifted a black leather folder. 'I've got papers for you to look at.'

Even Laura could sense Gaynor's excitement. Did John share it? she wondered.

So far Laura had been happy in her T-shirt and shorts, but when she saw Gaynor, in an obviously expensive pink linen dress with white shoes and hat, she felt plain and unfeminine.

'If we're going to talk business we'd better go somewhere more businesslike,' John said heavily. 'There's a table in my room. Jim, Laura, I'll see you later.'

For a moment his hand brushed the top of Laura's head. Then he was gone. Laura heard Gaynor's excited voice start at once. 'The studio chief has seen the videos you've made and...'

In spite of his openness, Laura knew there was a lot about John that she didn't know. She wasn't even sure about his character. He wasn't just the calm, easygoing, competent doctor most people saw. There was the tough, almost ruthless side which she'd seen once or twice. She did know that he'd had an affair with Gaynor and had even wanted to marry her.

Over the past few days she'd been opening herself more and more to him. She thought she was in love with him but now she wondered if all she was preparing for herself was pain. Perhaps she'd be better being wary.

Jim was sitting nearby, his dark face impassive. She wondered what he had made of Gaynor. She forced herself to try to forget the woman. Turning to Jim, she said, 'It's beautiful here. Do you ever get tired of it?'

He was a while replying, then he said, 'No. I was born and grew up in those mountains over there. And beyond is the mountain where First Woman gave the land to the Navajos. I was born in beauty. I wish to live in beauty.'

She looked at him curiously. 'Do you resent white people being here? Tourists wandering across your land?'

Once again he paused before replying. 'Navajos live in an impoverished land, but we are taught that everything should be shared—even our country.' There was another pause and then he said with a grin, 'I hope you don't think I am a simple red man. I speak four languages and I have a master's degree in anthropology from the University of New Mexico.'

'Sorry,' she said, feeling uncomfortably warm. 'I guess something like that had crossed my mind.'

'It doesn't matter.'

'Will you tell me more about the differences between Navajos and…white people?'

'Between the First People and the *biligaana*?' He smiled again. 'There are lots of differences. If you visit someone's hogan you wait outside till they are ready to see you. It is ill-mannered to announce yourself. You never interrupt someone when they are talking. And most important—you know that silences often say more than speech. If you talk too much you say less.'

Now she was sure he'd noticed her awkwardness with Gaynor. She felt a new respect for Jim Peyote.

'Are there many left, Jim?'

'Who still try to stick to the old ways? Quite a few.'

There was a further silence. She was getting used to it now and she discovered he was quite right. If you didn't talk too quickly you heard what other people had to say. It was a better way of communicating.

'The Navajo beliefs are based on *Hohzho*. It means harmony or beauty. Perhaps truth as well. They are the same. If you are wronged by someone then you do not demand punishment—you demand a return to *Hohzho*. The person who wronged you must recompense you, somehow right the wrong. There's no point in punishing him—that just doubles the lack of harmony. There must be harmony between nature and humanity, between the hunter and the hunted. The hunter may kill for food— but he must ask his prey's forgiveness and not kill just for sport. There must be harmony between man and woman.'

She was silent as she thought about this.

Jim went on, 'Illness is considered a form of disharmony. It's cured by a ceremony—chanting songs and painting pictures in coloured sand.' He smiled briefly. 'But when I had appendicitis I went to hospital.'

They sat in silence as the great golden ball of the sun sank behind the black mountains.

At first Laura thought she'd go straight to her room and to bed then she returned. Then she decided she'd avoided things too often in her life. It was time to face situations.

John and Gaynor were a long time in his room. The old Laura would have wondered if they were in bed together. Now, she fiercely told herself, she knew better. She had to learn to trust so she sat in the little staff common room and read magazines.

Finally they came out. Gaynor shook hands with her, smiled and said that she was sorry they'd not had chance to spend time together. Then she climbed into her large rented car. She wound down the window. 'You promised, John,' she shouted, 'so see you stick to your promise.' Then she was gone.

'I think I need a drink,' John said. 'Will you have one with me?'

She nodded and he fetched two glasses of white Zinfandel wine.

'Were you surprised to see Gaynor?' he asked. 'I certainly was.'

She remembered her conversation with Jim. Harmony, beauty and truth, he had said, were all the same. She would try to be truthful, even if it hurt.

'I was frightened,' she said. 'I thought she'd come for...for you.'

'And that upset you?'

It was the time for truth. 'Very much so,' she said. 'You know I've got quite...attached to you.'

'And did you think that I wasn't attached to you? Did you really think I'd leave you for her?'

'I don't think so—that is, I just don't know,' she said, bewildered. 'What about this job she's offered you? And what promise did you make?'

He sighed. 'Gaynor can be very persuasive. She made me promise not to make my mind up for at least a week. I've to think about it that long. I'll do that for her. The job is magnificent—half the time working in one of the great American hospitals, the other half making films for training in the Third World. Both well worthwhile.'

'You'd be foolish to turn it down,' Laura said miserably.

'I don't think so. There are more important things in life than work. You're one, Laura, I thought you knew that.'

'I do. Well, I think I do,' she said.

The next few days were busy. They went to the Carlsberg cavern, walked down into the depths and took a lift back. Unfortunately, they couldn't see the bat flights as the bats had all flown south. Jim took them to a rodeo. They went to Alamogordo and saw the white sands. The main road was closed for a while, and they sat outside the bus and watched a rocket streak off from the firing range.

There were one or two medical problems. Holidays were always a strain on ill young people, even though they'd had a rest halfway through. Brian Hughes's blood sugar level shot up for no apparent reason and John had difficulty in deciding the correct amount of insulin. In spite of frequent warnings and a daily inspection, two of the children managed to develop large blisters on their feet, which had to be dressed and kept under observation. There was a heated argument when Laura said they were *not* to go for a long walk with Jim Peyote.

Then finally it was time to go home. They were driven to El Paso airport—this time they were flying all the way back. Dwight, Helen and Jim said goodbye. Laura was sorry to part with them—they'd got quite close in the past few days. Some of the younger children were in tears.

Just before they boarded the plane John handed her a small box. 'From the Navajo nation,' he said.

She opened it. Inside were earrings in the traditional Navajo materials of silver and turquoise. Each was a silver ring with a filigree of silver wire inside. Tiny turquoise feathers hung from the bottom of the ring.

'They're called dream-catchers,' John said. 'They'll catch your dreams for you, Laura. Jim told me what to buy.'

'Do you know about my dreams, John?'

'I hope I do. I want you—us—to live in *Hohzho*. In harmony.'

'They're lovely,' she said. A small child banged into her—this wasn't the time for long speeches. 'But I don't think there'll be much harmony on this flight.'

In fact, it wasn't too bad. They flew to Orlando where they had to change planes and wait for an hour, then they took the overnight plane back to England.

Alice was restless and at first she wouldn't stop crying. There was nothing seriously wrong with her—she was over-tired and a little disorientated. Laura told John she'd stay by her. In time the little girl settled down and slept, her head against Laura's side.

Laura shut her eyes but couldn't sleep. That was unusual. She couldn't recollect having slept as well as she had over the past fortnight.

She had, she thought, really enjoyed the trip. She'd seen so much that was new and had had so many new experiences. It would take time for her to digest it all as it had happened so quickly. Of one thing she was certain. At some time she was going back to Texas and New Mexico.

But the holiday wasn't all of it. She'd spent a lot of

time with John. And she'd loved—well, nearly—every minute of it.

In the middle of the long mid-Atlantic flight Laura decided. She knew what she wanted. She'd go for it.

They lost five hours' sleep and arrived in Manchester early in the morning. Some children were collected by their parents and some would go straight to hospital for a check-up. Harry Roscoe was there to welcome them, and Laura and John were pleased to see him and to thank him.

She had the rest of the day off and went to her room in the nurses' home. She'd been warned that she'd suffer from jet-lag, a purely physiological reaction. In spite of her bodily tiredness there was a bright determination in her eyes. She'd changed. Soon people would see how much.

She'd been told not to go to bed till evening. The thing to do was to get used at once to the new time. After the two flights she felt quite grubby so she had a long bath and washed her hair. Then there was unpacking, her dirty washing to sort, little presents for Sal and her brothers to put ready. Then, dreading it, she went to see Robert. She'd sent him a couple of cards but had decided not to phone from America.

It had been Clive who'd told her that she had to leave Robert. 'You've helped us, Laura, but now we can cope. Go to America.'

Robert was propped up in bed, watching a television programme, and didn't look up as she approached. She glanced at the screen. A rugby match! Would he never learn? Then he looked up and she knew things were better. There was the cheeky grin, the old confident expression. Her irrepressible cousin was back, the fearful teenager had gone.

'Come here and give us a kiss, Larry,' he shouted. 'I've missed you.'

She bent to kiss him, wishing he could give her the bear-hug that always used to leave her breathless. 'You're more cheerful,' she said with a smile when finally she released him.

'Got something to be cheerful about. Look, Larry, small demonstration.' He nodded towards his hands. 'Watch,' he said.

She did as she was bidden and watched as, very, very slowly, his fingers clenched and unclenched.

'Not bad for a cripple, is it?' he asked. 'Hey, come on, you're supposed to cheer me up. Here, take one of my tissues and blow your nose.' Laura couldn't help it. Perhaps she was still jet-lagged. But all she could do was put her arms around him again and weep.

'You've got movement,' she said shakily after a while.

'Yes. Things aren't as bad as they seemed. Apparently, the nerve took a bashing but not as badly as they thought. I'm going to get better, Larry. It could take a year before I'm fit again, but I've got a year. I'll be able to walk and run and work. Even play rugby again.'

'Never!'

He grinned. 'That was a joke. Come on, Larry, I don't want emotion from you. I've had enough from Sal and the brothers. They've been a real gloomy lot. I expect you to be tough.'

'You expect me to be tough?'

'Everyone knows you're the tough one in the family. Who stopped us all falling apart when this happened? Who looked after Sal? You did.'

This was a totally new idea to her. 'Don't be silly,' she said cautiously.

'I'm not being silly.' He looked shamefaced. 'Larry, you saw me at my worst. You helped me when no one else could, talking about taking pills and so on.' He swallowed. 'Larry, if I ever get married, which is doubtful, and if I ever have kids, which at present I don't want, and if one is a girl—heaven forbid—I'll call her Laura. And I'll hope she'll be like you.'

'I suppose you think that's a compliment,' she said, 'so I'll take it as such. Here, I brought you a Miami Dolphins sweater.'

'Great!'

'And one thing more. I'm fed up with being called Larry. I don't want to be one of the boys—I'm a girl. From now on I'm Laura.'

'Whatever you say—Laura.' She liked it. It sounded good.

CHAPTER TEN

IT TOOK Laura three days to get back into the swing of things. There was the work on the ward to catch up on, a flying visit home to drop off presents and another photo-call for the local paper. She saw John only briefly—he was as busy as she was—but when she did see him he smiled and said, 'All this hard work. Was it worth going away?'

'I think so. Don't you?'

'I do, indeed. Just think, last week this time we were...' The photographer posed them for another picture.

But she would have a new beginning. When the jet-lag finally disappeared, and there seemed to be more to her future than just work, she sat on her bed and thought. For an hour she didn't move. Then she reached for a pen and pad and started to make notes. A new beginning. She'd start by phoning Sal.

'I'm at a bit of a loose end tonight, Sal. If you're going to the club I thought I might drop in for an hour and have a drink with you... Yes, it is a long time since we had a drink together. See you then.'

Her heart thumping, she rang off. Could she do it?

She didn't see John for three more days. He'd been in London for a meeting. The evening he returned she rang him. 'It's Wednesday,' she said. 'This may be a bit forward of me, but are you free next Saturday?' She could feel her heart racing again.

'Good to hear your voice, Laura. Yes, I'm free, not even on call. Any special reason?'

She took a breath. 'My treat. Would you like to come with me to the Gilmour Rugby Club? It's their pre-Christmas dinner and dance. You'd be a guest at my family's table.'

He didn't answer at once. Then he said, 'The rugby club. I thought it had unhappy memories for you, Laura.'

'It did have, but that's in the past. I'm starting a new life, John.'

'In that case, I would love to escort you. When shall I pick you up?'

Laura had the weekend free. At nine o'clock she met Sal in town. Saturday was usually the busiest day for a hairdresser, but Sal had taken it off.

She looked at Laura broodingly as they met in the middle of town. Laura was in her usual town clothes—anorak, trousers and light boots. Sal, however, was dressed in a smart green leather coat with matching beret. 'I take it you're not trying to make a point,' she said. 'Today we're shopping just for tonight. But if that's your idea of suitable clothing for town, well, we'd better come back next week and shop a bit more.'

'All right,' Laura said agreeably.

Sal looked surprised at her easy acquiescence. 'It's a date. Now, we need to start with the evening dress. We'll shop at Bailey's but there are three boutiques I'd like to check first.'

Laura was surprised at Sal's shrewdness. She had also never quite realised how difficult shopping for the right clothes could be. There were two or three dresses that she thought she might like, but Sal dismissed them all after an examination. 'Look at this lining. They've skimped on the material, and your skirt would bag after the first wearing.'

'I see,' Laura said.

Then there was a white dress which she thought might do. Sal scornfully dismissed it. 'It's pulled too tightly together at the top. Breathe heavily and your bust would pop out. This stitching is just not good enough.'

'I see,' Laura said again. For her, good stitching was what ensured a wound wouldn't bleed. She followed Sal to Bailey's where, she suspected, Sal had intended to go all the time.

Bailey's was big and expensive, the town's premier department store. It was a branch of a London shop, and the most Laura had ever bought there was a box of handkerchiefs.

Sal led the way. 'I know a girl in the gown section— I do her hair. She said she'd look out for us.' The 'girl' was called Mabel and she was about fifty. Her blue suit was immaculate and her blue-grey hair matched it. She and Sal looked at Laura critically.

'Good hair,' said Mabel. 'We'll have to find something to echo it.'

'I'm going to lighten it a bit this afternoon,' said Sal, 'but I think you're right. Take off that hideous coat, Laura.'

Laura did, and was subjected to another scrutiny. From her expression it was obvious that Mabel didn't much approve of thick sweaters either. 'Trim figure, too,' she said, 'and nice shoulders, I think. Just sit here and I'll fetch something for you.'

Laura had to admit that Mabel knew her job. She brought five dresses. Laura thought they were all ravishing. Sal inspected them more critically, holding them against Laura. Eventually she selected two, one a very dark red, the other midnight blue. 'We'll see these two on.'

It was a large and luxurious changing room where Laura undressed and pulled on the red dress. She looked in the mirror. The dress didn't go too well with her thick socks but she went outside anyway. Sal and Mabel pulled at the skirt, turned her this way and that. 'Not quite her eyes,' Mabel said eventually, and Sal agreed.

The blue dress rippled with changing colours from aquamarine to near black. It was strapless and deep cut at the front so when she put it on her bra showed. She went outside anyway. This was the dress she wanted—if she dared wear it.

'When did you buy your underwear, Laura? Nineteen forty-five?' Sal asked. 'Go and take that bra off. You've got a young girl's figure so make the most of it.'

She did as instructed. It was something she'd never done before. She felt vulnerable and yet knew she looked good. Sal and Mabel agreed. She was made to pirouette, walk, bend.

'Better line with heels,' Mabel said, and fetched a pair. 'Yes, that looks better.'

'How d'you fancy yourself?' Sal asked. 'Remember, with your own heels, reasonable tights and a new hair-style you'll be quite different.'

Laura looked apprehensively in the mirror. She knew she looked well but she'd never had a dress like this before. It was just not her. Then she decided. She was making a new beginning. She'd have a new dress. 'I'll have it,' she said.

With Sal she walked down the gold-painted stairs to the department below. 'I always wanted a daughter,' Sal said, 'and when I got you I was so pleased. But first you didn't like dolls and then when you grew up you didn't like clothes.' She turned and gave Laura a mock-serious frown. 'We're going to make up for lost time now. I think you'd better buy a coat.'

Half an hour later Laura had bought a dark blue leather coat. 'This will remain fashionable for years,' Sal said, 'and it suits your colouring. We'll go for a coffee. I haven't enjoyed myself so much in years.'

They sat, sipping coffee from dainty cups and eating tiny chocolate crisps. 'So, are you happy with what you've bought so far?' Sal asked.

'Yes. Just a bit apprehensive. It's not really what I've been used to.'

'You'll get used to it,' Sal said, 'and you've no idea how much this means to me. Now, here's something for you.' She slid an old leather jewellery box across the table. Laura opened it. It held a chain of alternate gold and silver links. It was obviously old, and she thought she'd never seen anything so lovely.

'It was my grandmother's,' Sal said. 'Then it was my mother's and then mine. Now it's for you. It'll go well with the blue dress.'

Laura pushed the box back across the table. 'I can't take it,' she said. 'It's yours.'

Sal pushed it back again. 'I've got plenty of jewellery. I suspect you've got none. I want you to have it, Laura. It's still in the family.'

Laura hesitated, then picked up the box. 'Thank you,' she said.

There was more shopping. First of all an evening bag, then three pairs of tights, not in her customary service-able brown but sheer and shimmery. Sal chose for her a pair of simple black shoes, but with the highest heels she'd ever worn. 'You need heels with that dress,' Sal

said. 'Trust me.' Then came a silk stole in a comple-
mentary shade of light blue.

'Last of all is underwear,' Sal said, leading Laura
down a further set of steps. 'I'm sure what you've got
is serviceable, but for a special occasion you need something special. Romantic even. You want to feel gorgeous
from the skin outwards.'

'No one's going to see it but me,' Laura protested,
using an ancient argument.

'Are you sure?'

Laura didn't answer, but blushed a rosy red.

'What I mean,' said Sal expressionlessly, 'is that you
might be in an accident.'

'Those look nice over there,' Laura said wildly. In the
end she bought four matching sets of silk underwear at
what she thought was a ludicrous price.

They'd spent three hours in Bailey's before they could
walk out, carrying the distinctive shiny grey carrier bags.
'That was enjoyable,' Sal said with considerable satis-
faction. 'Now, this afternoon…'

At nearly eight that night Laura sat in the bedroom
where she'd spent so much of her childhood. She felt
apprehensive, almost bewildered. She hadn't realised
that being beautiful took so much trouble—or could be
so much fun. At Sal's Salon—that was its name—she'd
had a body treatment, a manicure and a pedicure. Sal
herself had cut, restyled and tinted her hair. There was
more of her face visible now, her cheekbones were ac-
centuated and she thought she looked, well, more clas-
sical.

Then she'd had a face make-over. Sal's expert had
helped her select new make-up, and had carefully explained how various elements should be combined.

She wore both the gold and silver necklace Sal had given her and the earrings from John. Never before had she worn so much jewellery—she seldom wore any— but she had to admit the two looked well together.

Laura stared in the mirror at the result and a new face looked back at her. It was the face of a confident, sophisticated woman. She hoped she had the character, the new personality, to match.

There was a shout from downstairs. 'Taxi at the front door, Laura. I think it's your guest. You let him in.' For a moment she didn't want to move. She wanted to stay in her own room where she'd been happy in her shell. Then she forced herself to walk downstairs, and answer the doorbell. Only she was in the hall when she opened the door.

John stood there, a sheaf of flowers under his arm. She'd never seen him in a dinner jacket before and the flattering contrast of black and white suited him. He smiled, but even in the dimness of the porch light she could see a hint of wariness in his eyes. He's worried about me, she thought, and the thought pleased her.

'Good to see you, John,' she said, and leaned forward to kiss him—not a dainty air kiss, but one that left lipstick on his cheek. She brought him into the brightness of the hall and thrilled at the incredulous look he gave her. 'You're gorgeous,' he breathed, 'more lovely than ever.'

'It's all Sal's doing, just for the night. I'll be plain Sister McLeod again next week.'

'You'll never be plain.' They stood in silence for a moment. Each felt there were things to be said but this was to be a family—a social—occasion.

'Come and meet everybody,' she said, taking his arm.

'Yes, but first...' From behind the large bouquet of

flowers he took a box, holding a single white orchid.
'This is for you.'

'Oh, it's lovely,' she said, and impulsively kissed him
again. This time he took her waist and held her a minute.

The large bouquet was for Sal, who was delighted.
Not a lot of men in her family brought her flowers. John
shook hands with Clive and Colin, accepted a drink and
one of what Sal called 'small, hot thingies'. Within
minutes he'd been accepted. As the men talked, Sal drew
Laura to one side so she could pin the orchid on her
dress. 'He's a nice man,' she said. 'Thoughtful. Are
you...close?'

'Well, I like him a lot,' Laura said.

The rugby club was within walking distance, and it
was traditional that the family never drove there. John
held her arm as they entered the gates. 'Is this going to
be an ordeal?' he asked.

'No, John. I'm here to enjoy myself.'

'Good.' After a moment's companionable silence he
said, 'I phoned Gaynor Gladstone this afternoon. I didn't
think it fair to keep her waiting.'

'About the job?' Laura asked, trying to sound no more
than vaguely curious.

'Yes. She wasn't very pleased when I turned it down.
I told her I had too much to do up here.'

'Well, I'm glad. You're too good a doctor to lose.'

'I wasn't only thinking of being a doctor.' They
walked through the brightly lit doorway.

There was a moment of initial apprehension. The last
time she'd come to an affair like this she'd... But there
was no need to worry. She was older, more mature. She
was also surprised at how many people remembered her,
said hello and how they hoped to see her again. Sal's

table had a succession of visitors and it gave her pleasure to introduce John.

It was a good evening. John insisted on buying champagne for the table. The meal was simple but good, and Sal told people that she wouldn't smoke—she was trying to cut down anyhow. When Laura danced with John she felt she was in heaven.

Yes, it was a very good evening. Mostly she danced with John, but there were other claimants. She wondered why she'd kept away from affairs like this—she was enjoying herself so much. Then she recalled why, and shuddered. That was behind her.

The dance was to end at one. John said he'd ordered a taxi. Laura thought a minute and then asked Sal if she minded if she went back to the hospital with John. Sal said, 'You enjoy yourself, honey.'

Then it was the last dance. Couples swirled slowly round the floor and, like every other woman, Laura leaned against her partner as his arms met around her. At the end she looked up and said, 'May I come back with you?'

He looked slightly surprised. 'Aren't you staying with your family?'

'Not tonight. It's been lovely, being with them—and with you—but there are things I've got to do.'

'Then you're very welcome.'

There was a round of farewells, promises to meet again soon, a special hug from Sal. 'You don't know how happy it's made me, having you here with us.'

'I'll be back soon, Sal.' Then John was at the doorway, beckoning. The taxi had arrived.

After the noise and conviviality of the dance it was pleasant to sit in the dark with John's arm gently round her. 'I don't need to ask if you enjoyed yourself,' he whispered, and she squeezed his hand.

She hadn't had too much to drink and she'd noticed that John had also drunk little. As they neared the hospital she wished she'd had a little more—she needed some artificial courage. When he leaned forward to direct the taxi driver she managed to speak. 'I don't want to go home just yet. Please, would you like to make me a coffee at your flat?'

'Of course,' he said easily, and gave the driver the address. She leaned back in her seat and breathed out. She had managed it.

In his living room Laura sat in the deep leather couch while he pottered in the kitchen. 'I've just bought a new CD,' he said. 'See what you think.'

It was Ella Fitzgerald, and the track was 'Every time you say goodbye I die a little'. Had he chosen that track deliberately? she wondered. Whatever, she reacted to the beauty of it, to the world-weariness in the voice. She kicked off her shoes and leaned back. She was tired—and exhilarated at the same time.

When John came back with the silver coffee-tray she saw he'd taken off his jacket and bow-tie. The whiteness of his shirt showed up his strong brown neck. 'Men are lucky,' she said. 'They can relax so easily.' She waved a fold of her skirt at him. 'This is my new dress and I love it, but it's not designed for sprawling on couches.'

He sat next to her and poured the coffee. 'I think it's a lovely dress,' he said. 'It even matches the couch. But I'll lend you something if you want. I was in Hong Kong a couple of years ago for a conference. I bought a silk dressing-gown but I've never dared wear it.'

Silence stretched between them. 'All right,' she said.

He took her into the spare bedroom, pulled a box from a wardrobe and dropped it on the bed. 'Leave you to it.'

She opened the box and drew aside layers of tissue paper. There it was, in brilliant red and silver with a broad black band around every hem. For a moment she stood in thought, her lower lip clenched between her teeth. Then she carefully slid out of her blue dress. Not daring to look at her near nakedness in the large mirror, she put on the dressing-gown and belted it tightly round her. Then she turned.

'Look,' she said as she re-entered the living room. She held her arms out straight sideways. The broad sleeves fell from her elbows, forming a giant T.

'I'm tired of saying it,' he murmured huskily, 'but you look gorgeous. Now, come and have your coffee.'

She sank back onto the couch beside him and drank from her cup. The CD had come to an end, and there was a 'ting' when she replaced her cup that rang out in the silence. He slid his arm around her neck and she closed her eyes with a tiny smile as he leaned over and kissed her. She could feel the throbbing of her heart as his lips roved over her face, touching, teasing and nibbling, till she reached out and pulled him closer. His kiss became more urgent, more demanding, and as she felt the hardness of him her lips parted.

His hand moved down the front of her gown, easing away the folds of silk until his hand gently cupped her breast. She felt the tension mount inside her and gripped his arm. Suddenly the panic was gone and she sighed. Everything would be all right.

His head dipped as he pushed her gown aside, and she cried aloud as his mouth touched and then enveloped each aroused peak in turn. Her hands reached for the front of his shirt, pulling at the buttons so she could caress the muscle underneath and feel the warmth of his body. When he crushed her against him she felt the infinitely exciting rasp of hair against her.

Her gown dropped, and she was naked to the waist, sitting in a pool of red silk. He kissed her again then stood and offered her his hands in a wordless gesture. She also rose and, his arm round her waist, led her to his bed.

At first she was happy to let him explore her body, but soon she grew bold, and revelled in what she could do—the sighs and moans of delight she could cause. They were matched by her own. Then she felt his mounting need for her and somehow she knew what to do. There was one tiny moment of pain and then she was with him. Their bodies joined in a primeval rhythm, an ecstasy of feeling that led through a whirlwind of sensation to the final sweet cry of culmination.

'That was nice,' she sighed.

John lay on his back, one arm round Laura's waist. She was half on top of him with her head cradled on his shoulder. After the delirium of passion they seemed to want to talk and share a different kind of togetherness.

With her fingertips she traced a line down his forehead, his nose and the sweet sweet curve of his lips. She could smell his warmth, his maleness, mixed with her own body scent.

'I love you,' he said.

'I know you love me. And I love you, too. It's part of the new life I'm starting.'

His hand stroked deliciously from her nape down her back. 'Am I part of your new life?'

'You're more than the most important part—you're all of it,' she said drowsily. 'You shouldn't do that. I like it.'

'So, will you marry me?'

She rubbed her leg over his. 'Try and stop me,' she said, and thought the occasion merited another kiss.

'There's a lot about you I don't know,' she went on some time later, 'and I want to know everything.'

'I'll tell you whatever you ask.'

'Well, there's Gaynor for a start. It's difficult 'cos I quite like her, but she'll be disappointed that you're not going to work for her. And I think she still— Well, you did say you thought of marrying her.'

He pulled her down to him and quickly kissed her again. 'Gaynor is the complete professional. Once she realises she can't have me, working for her, she'll find someone else. As for any closer personal feelings, well, I hadn't met you then. Gaynor I liked. But I love you. And the difference is infinite.'

It was so good to hear him say so. But... 'And don't you mind, not making films, not going to work in America?'

He shook his head. 'My work is here. I like the area, the hospital, the people I work with. I'm even acquiring a ready-made family. Sal is wonderful.'

Laura knew Sal was wonderful—now more than ever. 'That's another thing. You've met my family and they all like you. It makes me so happy. But will your parents like me? I'm taking their only son.'

'My parents will love you. I told you that somehow we've drifted apart. It was no one's fault really, but it happened. And lately we've all felt it, and I know we've wondered what we can do—how we can turn into a normal family. So I've come up with a solution. Grandchildren!'

'Grandchildren!' she squeaked.

'You'll be a fabulous mother. And it might be sooner

than you think. Did you notice I didn't use any precautions?'

No, she hadn't noticed. Hastily she started to calculate. 'I think we're all right,' she said after a moment.

'I don't want us to be all right. I want you to have babies. One of each, and the third you can decide on.'

'You can't order them just like that,' she said with a grin.

'Well, I'll make do with whatever you offer me.' His hand reached to cup her breast, which was gently grazing his chest. 'In fact, shall we try again now?'

She gasped with pleasure as his thumb caressed the pink, erect peak.

'Soon,' she whispered. 'Soon.'

'Very soon.' But he made no move. Both of them were happy just to be together.

'It's good news about Robert,' John went on after a while. 'I dropped in to see him after I'd had a chat with Charles Whitrow a couple of days ago. Charles is delighted—and surprised. Every now and again something happens that confounds all medical knowledge. I think it's a good thing. Keeps us from getting too confident.'

She shivered. 'It was a miracle. And he needed one. Robert in a wheelchair would have been unthinkable.'

'D'you think he'll be well enough to hold a ring? With no brother of my own, I'll need to borrow one to be best man.'

'Oh, John!' She hugged him harder, if possible, than she had done so far.

He hugged her back. And, slowly this time, he eased her onto her back.

His touch was delicate at first, and she lay back, letting him do with her what he would. Like waves, lapping on a beach, the pleasure took her and surged through her in slow, sensual repetition. This must be the new me, Laura thought. I wouldn't—couldn't—have felt like this a month ago. She gave herself to him fully, knowing now that all her giving would be returned—a hundredfold.

MILLS & BOON®

Makes any time special

Enjoy a romantic novel from Mills & Boon®

Presents™ *Enchanted*™ *Temptation*®

Historical Romance™ *Medical Romance*™

MILLS & BOON®

Medical Romance™

COMING NEXT MONTH

VILLAGE PARTNERS by Laura MacDonald

Dr Sara Denton tried to forget Dr Alex Mason, but it didn't work. Then she went to her uncle's and found Alex was a partner at the general practice! And Alex *really* wanted her to stay...

ONE OF A KIND by Alison Roberts

Dr Sam Marshall, fresh from Australia, was certainly unique! Sister Kate Campbell, with an A&E department to run at the busy London hospital, had no time to spare, but Sam was persistent!

MARRYING HER PARTNER by Jennifer Taylor
A Country Practice—the first of four books.

Dr Elizabeth Allen wasn't comfortable with change, but when Dr James Sinclair arrived at the Lake District practice, change was inevitable!

ONE OF THE FAMILY by Meredith Webber

Nurse Sarah Tremaine wanted to adopt baby Sam, but first she had to get permission from the child's uncle. But Dr Adam Fletcher didn't know he had a nephew...

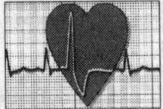

Available from 7th May 1999

MILLS & BOON®

Next Month's Romance Titles

♡

Each month you can choose from a wide variety of romance novels from Mills & Boon®. Below are the new titles to look out for next month from the Presents™ and Enchanted™ series.

Presents™

THE SPANISH GROOM	Lynne Graham
HER GUILTY SECRET	Anne Mather
THE PATERNITY AFFAIR	Robyn Donald
MARRIAGE ON THE EDGE	Sandra Marton
THE UNEXPECTED BABY	Diana Hamilton
VIRGIN MISTRESS	Kay Thorpe
MAKESHIFT MARRIAGE	Daphne Clair
SATURDAY'S BRIDE	Kate Walker

Enchanted™

AN INNOCENT BRIDE	Betty Neels
NELL'S COWBOY	Debbie Macomber
DADDY AND DAUGHTERS	Barbara McMahon
MARRYING WILLIAM	Trisha David
HIS GIRL MONDAY TO FRIDAY	Linda Miles
BRIDE INCLUDED	Janelle Denison
OUTBACK WIFE AND MOTHER	Barbara Hannay
HAVE BABY, WILL MARRY	Christie Ridgway

On sale from 7th May 1999

H1 9904

Available at most branches of WH Smith, Tesco, Asda, Martins, Borders, Easons, Volume One/James Thin and most good paperback bookshops

2 FREE
books and a surprise gift!

We would like to take this opportunity to thank you for reading this Mills & Boon® book by offering you the chance to take TWO more specially selected titles from the Medical Romance™ series absolutely FREE! We're also making this offer to introduce you to the benefits of the Reader Service™—

- ★ FREE home delivery
- ★ FREE gifts and competitions
- ★ FREE monthly Newsletter
- ★ Exclusive Reader Service discounts
- ★ Books available before they're in the shops

Accepting these FREE books and gift places you under no obligation to buy, you may cancel at any time, even after receiving your free shipment. Simply complete your details below and return the entire page to the address below. *You don't even need a stamp!*

YES! Please send me 2 free Medical Romance books and a surprise gift. I understand that unless you hear from me, I will receive 4 superb new titles every month for just £2.40 each, postage and packing free. I am under no obligation to purchase any books and may cancel my subscription at any time. The free books and gift will be mine to keep in any case.

M9EA

Ms/Mrs/Miss/Mr ....Initials................................
BLOCK CAPITALS PLEASE

Surname ....

Address ....

....

....Postcode ....

Send this whole page to:
THE READER SERVICE, FREEPOST CN81, CROYDON, CR9 3WZ
(Eire readers please send coupon to: P.O. BOX 4546, DUBLIN 24.)

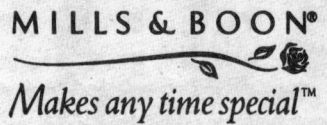

The Regency Collection

Mills & Boon® is delighted to bring back, for a limited period, 12 of our favourite Regency Romances for you to enjoy.

These special books will be available for you to collect each month from May, and with two full-length Historical Romance™ novels in each volume they are great value at only £4.99.

Volume One available from 7th May